For Cain

It is the year 2989 in the lan
of the world. King Mindsley,
democratic leader is trying to keep the vicious and aggressive Lizard race; The Lacertians, at bay while simultaneously keeping his subjects from falling into division and hostility towards one another. There are mages on either side conjuring all types of magic to destroy the opposing side. It's fucking epic!

In the Southern city, at Verrenum castle the King is discussing strategy with his council in regards to the oncoming Lacertian invasion.

"The Lacertians have reached Ventricala, King. The battle between the mortals has begun. We have battalions of men and orcs in the North, here, here and here. The Elves have sent troops to fight and guard the southern part." Said Rook Graipaint; the highest and closest of King Mindsley's advisors.
"And the borderlands? If they find a route through the forests they could invade either one of the cities. And the towns, the places in between. I won't allow the small communities to be at any more risk than us." The king replied, pointing to the places on the map in front of him.
Rook Graipaint paused before answering, not wanting to be loose with his tongue and appear foolish as those who don't think before they speak do. He looked hard at the map in silence, then he replied. "They

wouldn't risk it would they? The land would consume them, surely!"
The council stared at the map and all paused in contemplation, thinking deeply about their actions because of the severity of mistakes made in warfare. If they failed in their decisions then the repercussions would be catastrophic not only for themselves but for all the people of Verrenum. The Lacertians would butcher and enslave the people. They would burn everything in their path and leave Verrenum a grey land of ash.
"The land has clearly marked where we sentient beings are allowed to travel. The Ventricala path must be the only way they could enter Verrenum. Don't you think?" Rook Graipaint asked.
"I don't know." King Mindsley replied, "The Lacertians have attacked and failed before. I wouldn't put it past King Gila to try something else this time."
"Maybe we should get advice from one of the mages on this, King." One of the King's Bishops said.
"Yes, that's a good idea, should I send for Mehinnerst?" The Rook asked.
"Yes, ask him to come. Don't order him. He won't like it." The king answered, in his democratic fashion. He had never liked giving orders, preferring to treat his subjects as his equals, and they respected him for it. His lack of tyranny had always benefited himself, and those around him. He found that people were much more productive when they were treated with dignity and respect, rather than being ordered around like sheep.

"Ofcourse." Rook Graipaint replied.

In the most Northern part of Lacertia, there is the biggest building ever built in all of the world. It is the biggest, for a reason, The extremely egotistical King Gila wouldn't have himself be out done by any of the other kings he is descended from, or any other creature. Every Lacertian king had either knocked their predecessor's castle down or just simply added more to it.
The intimidating structure is created from the black volcanic rock of the coast, at the end of a sharp point on the land and covered from the ground to the tip of the tallest tower where King Gila stays, with the most fearful artwork of statues, hideous gargoyles and celebrations of King Gila's history of torture carved into the stone like a story so that every being that looks upon it will know of what he considers his greatest achievements.
King Gila, as well as his predecessors have the philosophy of being as ruthless, tyrannical, strong and as feared as possible. They believe in the most severe torture for anyone disloyal to them. In their eyes, since their God; the overlord, allows it, torture is not only completely justified but expected as a sign of goodness. To torture is to be like God in their eyes, as God is the most torturous of all beings.
All must outdo the last king in every one of the Lacertian's passions. None of the previous King's have managed to successfully invade Verrenum, but

that won't stop the ambitious and obsessive King Gila from trying.

"The battle at Ventricala has begun my King." One of King Gila's bishops declared. Immediately, the King's Rook Kawmdo swung his sword and cut off the bishop's head, dropping the Lacertian to the floor with a loud thud. Foolishly, he believed this would get him more in the king's favour, but Gila just saw it as an insult; as if he couldn't have done it himself! The king turned to his guards in the room and emotionlessly ordered, "Take the Rook Kawmdo to Blairack."
The Rook, stunned by this, suddenly saw his mistake, and his head stared down towards the floor. Thinking, contemplating on why this must be. What great lesson was the Overlord trying to teach him? There must be a higher reason for his folly. He stayed silent, and dared not to look the King in his reptilian eyes in case Gila saw defiance in his own. He went quietly with the guards as they gripped him with their clawed hands, beginning his journey to the notorious prison of the Lizard King.
"Take the bishop's body as well." The king said, pointing to the corpse on the floor.
"But leave the head. Pass it to me!" Gila ordered, and he took the head from a guard and put it in the grimacing face of every other Lacertian there.
"This is what will happen to you if you think you are smarter than me and try to tell me something I already know. Of course I know the battle has begun. Also, and I don't understand why the curse you lot haven't

understood this yet but never look me in the eye and NEVER speak to me unless I request you too!" The King grabbed the chin of one of his bishop's. He moved his scaled face closer, his forked tongue moving in and out and concluded, "Do you understand?" There was fire in his eyes. His jaw clenched with tremendous muscle. He was terrifying to all of them.

"Yes King." Every Lacertian in the room replied.

Gila made sure the bishop wouldn't return his intimidating eye contact and then promoted him to Rook.

"You will take Kawmdo's place as Rook."

"Yes King." The new Rook, Horridum replied.

"Now, situated right above the Ventricala pass is the Verrenum borderlands. While the battle rages, and it will be raging for years, I believe we should, I should!" The king corrected himself before continuing, "Attempt something no other Lacertian has and find a safe route to take another army through the borderlands and into Verrenum." King Gila began, and his finger and sharp claw trailed the map in a circular motion.

"Once we have found a safe route through, we will establish a road where we can send a constant flow of armies to attack the Southern city from behind the Verrenum's lines, and ultimately kill King Mindsley."

The room was completely silent. King Gila began laughing coarsely.

"A good idea? Rook Horridum?" He stated while backhanding the Rook Horridum on the chest cracking the silence.

"Yes King. Perfect!" The Rook replied.
"Anything to add to it?" King Gila asked.
"No my king. Your judgement is that of The Overlord himself." Rook Horridum answered swiftly.
"Good!" The king retorted. Smiling for the first time during the meeting, revealing his sharpened teeth like that of a shark.
"Operation Roadkill we will call it, but who will lead them? I want our finest warriors of those who aren't already on the frontlines. Do any of you have any ideas?" The king asked.
The bishops and Rook Horridum stayed quiet knowing that Gila would take offence if any of them mentioned something and therefore assumed he in all his might and wisdom couldn't have thought of it himself.
"We will grant immunity to those who win in gladiator games at Blairack!" The king blurted out, still smiling and in love with the ideas flowing through his superior brain. The brain that was ordained by the Overlord to lead all of Lacertia, and all the world once it was conquered.
"We will give them all a chance to win back their freedom and take part in Operation Roadkill. Bishop Salvator, you will take my orders to the guards at Blairack and watch over the games. Do what you will to bring me back the finest of the damned. I want 400 Lizards for this, and document it all as well so that the population will hear of my...actually wait." The king paused in contemplation, then spoke his thoughts out loud. "Am I being too merciful? Does it even matter if I am? Why should I question anything I do when

nobody else would dare!? Has the Overlord not chosen me, Gila, to be the ultimate leader of all of the Lacertian's?"
The King turned and stared hard out of the window, peering at the view of his surrounding city and all the Lacertians that were beneath him, and it suddenly dawned on him how high up he was.
"Document it!" The king exclaimed and turned back to his henchmen, "Use it as propaganda. The population will see that I have managed to kill two birds with one stone, to make fuel for the fire out of shit! and all Lacertia will admire me even more, for my genius."

Mehinnerst was favoured over the other mages King Mindsley had living with him in his castle. The wizard was skilled in warfare and bounty hunting for the King and he had much experience in both. He was also extremely powerful. Many argued that he was the most powerful mage alive. Others saw that just as propaganda though. That he was a sell out. A sycophant. And that there were many mages in the poorer areas who were just as powerful, if not more, but just hadn't been chosen as Mehinnerst had; they just didn't have the opportunities and so nobody noticed them.
What was definitely true though, was that Mehinnerst worked hard with what he had, and he practiced magic on a regular basis, trying to gain as much knowledge of it as possible. He spent much of his time reading in the library, practicing spells, creating potions and preparing for warfare. He enjoyed it, and

he was dedicated to the assignments given to him. He put in as much effort as possible in his every action, always in constant motion, trying to better himself, trying to master the Infinite as much as he could. He believed in Verrenum, and he believed in King Mindsley. He was dedicated to the ideas of the time and felt obliged to do his best regardless of whether or not he was rewarded for it, but he was - rewarded that is; he was very blessed, and very rich.

He was deep in study at the royal library when he was called for by a messenger for the council, and as he walked to see King Mindsley, through the beautiful gothic architecture of Verrenum castle, he got a sudden surge of adrenaline, as if this next mission of his would be his greatest one. A premonition. A strong one. The thought of it made his body toughen itself. He could feel the bones grow denser, his muscles tighten and his skin turn firmer as he passed down the halls of the castle and finally entered the King's court where the council were talking over the map of Verrenum.

"Ah, Mehinnerst. It's good to see you." The King said, approaching the wizard and shaking his hand.

"Come in, please, I could use your council."

Mehinnerst followed the king and stood by the table as the bishops made room for him. They were trusting of the mage because he had not let the King down before, but still weary of him. Men had always feared his power so he took no offence to it. His eyes eagerly darted around the map and he listened intently to catch up as the council continued.

"King Mindsley believes that Gila may attempt to find a route through the borderlands in order to attack Verrenum." Rook Graipaint said.
"That's unlikely." Mehinnerst Replied, "I don't think the land would allow it. We have a great country here in Verrenum. The Infinite surely must favour us to continue as we are."
"Is it possible?" King Mindsley asked.
"Anything is possible." Mehinnerst answered.
The King looked at the wizard intriguingly and Mehinnerst noticed it so he continued, "Well there is the Ghost town of the Claudian forest which we know of. Many criminals have exited the eastern city and fled there. The land has allowed them to set up somewhat of a village, at a cost; their numbers are culled by the Nosferatu who dwell there also. I can think of no others who have not been consumed by the land though. Apart from the wizard Ackley."
"Who is this Ackley?" The King asked.
"He was a vagabond, a brigand, an anarchist. He was always in trouble in some way or another until he just changed his ways completely. He left the cities and wandered off into the borderlands to live as a recluse. A lot venture into it, but he, as far as I know, is the only one who has survived and returned. He lives a few miles into the forest, just above the crossroads on the eastern city road. I think! I mean, that was the last place he stayed. He may have moved since then. He could help us with this, whether he will or not is another question. He has no interest in the common ways of bribery." Mehinnerst answered.

"How could he help us?" The Rook Graipaint asked, trusting the wizard's judgement but wanting to know more.
"Well he knows the borderlands better than anyone else I can think of. He may give us an answer on whether the Lacertian's could get through and if so, what they would need to do. I mean, there are ancient things in the forests, and nature that we cannot even comprehend. Creatures and magic that none of us can even imagine. It's like an ocean." Mehinnerst answered.
"I want you to go to him." The King Commented, "I want you to take whichever of your wizards with you, find him and if possible, get him to Ventricala to guide you through the borderlands to make sure the Lacertian's have not found a way through. I'll send an army in a few weeks especially trained for this mission to meet you at Ventricala. If, for whatever reason the wizard Ackley will not help us then I want you to find another who will or, guide them yourself."
"King, I've never even been into the Borderlands. I know only from informers in the cities of Ghost town and Ackley. He may not even exist in the way he is described. It could be falsehoods." The wizard explained.
"Are you declining the mission?" Rook Graipaint asked.
"No, I'm just telling you every detail so you can make an informed decision." Mehinnerst answered.
"Take some soldiers with you." The Rook said.

"They would need to be expendable!" Mehinnerst retorted, which made the whole room laugh.
"I'm up for it King, but the chances are slim that we will come back if we go into the borderlands, or even find the wizard Ackley. I will do this for Verrenum, ofcourse! I just want you to know what the risks are. The land isn't always kind to those who wish to rule it. Unless it sees this as necessary for the future of Verrenum then it will probably kill us all." Mehinnerst explained.
"Do you think it is worth the risk?" King Mindsley asked, respecting his mage rook's opinion, "I wouldn't want you to die without reason."
The wizard paused for a few seconds going over it in his mind before answering unwaveringly.
"Yes. Plus I have always wanted a reason to enter the borderlands. Without an important one it would surely kill me. I have had dreams from it warning me to stay away when hunting fugitives before."
Mehinnerst saw them in his mind running into the dark forests, only to be consumed by it over time. The land was alive, and it used them for various purposes. They were all just puppets to it.
"Only one of my wizards has ever been in and that was only to Ghost Town to spy on what it has become. I would like to see the borderlands for myself though." Mehinnerst explained.
"Then go, and take whatever you need to bribe the wizard Ackley." King Mindsley said.
"We'll see you at Ventricala in a few weeks." Rook Graipaint concluded.

And so the wizard Mehinnerst left, to gather up what he needed for the journey.

Kawmdo was pacing back and forth in the prison cell within Gila castle he was being held in before being transferred to Blairack, wondering why, and trying to stay empty and not let his anger best him. He saw a use for anger of course, but in times like these he believed it was best to stay vigilant, and empty. He couldn't tell the other Lacertian's this. It was not their ways, and he would be accused of being a traitor for having this mentality.
The Lacertian's were meant to be violent and vengeful, angry and greedy, but Kawmdo had realised that to be like this all the time would most likely lead to his destruction. These emotions were like fire and could fuel him if they were managed correctly but if he let the fires blaze he felt that they would consume him.
"I'm being transferred to Blairack!" He said to himself in his head and his hand rubbed his forehead.
"Transferred!" A voice came from the darkest corner of the room, "Transferred! You mean trafficked! Kidnapped! Murdered!" It continued.
Kawmdo jolted back and took a violent stance, lifting his fists up. He stayed quiet, just peering into the dark, until the white face of a woman with a huge black smile which looked as if it had been stained on with smoke began appearing.
"You're a homo sapien!" Kawmdo commented, shocked by the fact she wasn't a Lacertian.

"Not quite!" She replied as she creeped out of the shadows like an arachnid, "I mean, I was human. Long ago. They burnt me though." She stated.
She twirled as she moved around the cell and went to the corner where she then leaned up to a cobweb and let the spider crawl down her hand.
"Once upon a time, like you, I was the fly!" She whispered, and then turned to face the Lacertian who was still ready to attack, his mind racing with thoughts.
"I love your mind, Lacertian. Constantly contemplating the best way. It's revolutionary! It's a shame King Gila couldn't see it." She said.
"What do you want from me?" Kawmdo asked.
"I want to set you free." She answered and sat down on the black volcanic floor, letting the spider string its gossamer around her fingers. She dangled it and looked completely obsessed with it for a second.
Kawmdo stayed silent, waiting for her to explain.
"I want to set you free from that tyrant! Of this place! I know you have grown weary of it. He's cursed you over pretty bad, they all have." She explained.
Kawmdo thought of his people. He saw them in his mind, drinking the blood of their enemies. He thought of how violent they were and how quick they were to kill those who insulted them, and he thought about how perfect they were, and he stared back at the woman twisting his head as a dog does when it is confused.
Then he swiftly rushed towards her. He gripped her by the throat, lifting her up, scraping her against the

jagged wall, revealing his teeth, ready to bite into her throat but she screamed and disappeared.
"Kawmdo!" A guard shouted, standing at the prison cell door.
"What?" He scorned, turning to face him.
The guard saw the rage in his eyes and felt a chill jolt through his cold blood.
"Who was that?" The guard asked in a more politeful manner.
"Just a witch. A Verrenum spy. Telling lies! Trying to get me to turn against Lacertia. Astral projection I think they call it. Trying to curse with my head." The lizard replied and he turned towards the guard. He stood up straight.
"Are you taking me to Blairack?" He asked.
"Yes." The guard sternly replied.
"Then let's go." Kawmdo said, and he walked to the door as the guard nodded in approval, impressed by the ex rooks dedication to the Overlord and his will.
"Kawmdo began to feel a rush of excitement. The most notorious prison in all of Lacertia! He paced ahead of the guards, past the other Lacertian's in their cells. Some looked afraid. Others stared at him aggressively which made him laugh at their ridiculousness, their immaturity.
He was moved from the castle to the outside where curiously it was raining, a rare occurrence in Lacertia. The monsoon had arrived. He stared up at the sky trying to capture a glimpse of the overlord in clouds as he was guided towards the carriage filled with other prisoners, ready to take them to their destination.

Mehinnerst came to the door of his Rookess; Francine, and knocked three times. The huge door opened seemingly by itself and he went inside.
The room was dark, as the windows were covered in black cloth to keep out the daylight. Mehinnerst didn't particularly like the ways of Francine, she was much more into darker magic than he was, but whatever she did, it did work. She was an important part of their team.
Her powers as a witch were pretty much unrivalled amongst those in the Southern city. She wasn't very well liked there though which is why she kept herself to herself. Having revealed that she could read minds had its bonuses yes, but it also came with a lot of drawbacks. Other beings of Verrenum, especially the humans, didn't like to be around her very often.
That's why she preferred darkness and the company of insects, for when she read their minds they never cared. They were a lot more transparent creatures than the mortals. They didn't pretend because of social pressures. They didn't try to hide what they were. They were selfish, ruthless hunters which she admired in them and tried to emulate in her work for Mehinnerst, the King, and most importantly: Verrenum.
She had second guessed her revelation of psychic ability at times, but no matter how she was treated by some of the people of Verrenum, she loved the land and had always been quite independent anyway so it didn't bother her much. She understood she had

evolved to be a more solitary being. She felt obliged though, as did Mehinnerst, to protect Verrenum, to fight for it and use her powers given to her by the infinite in the way in which she saw fit.

Mehinnerst walked to the table which was covered in a mess of open spell books and potions. A rat scurried across it and hid as the wizard approached.
"You have no need to fear him." The witch communicated to the rat who came out of the shadows just as she did.
"So, what is the news from King Mindsley?" Francine asked.
Mehinnerst recalled what had been said in the meeting and the witch viewed and heard it all in his mind within seconds.
"Oh, this is exciting! You have always wanted a good enough reason to enter the borderlands!" Francine said.
"Yes." Mehinnerst Replied, "But it has always warned me to stay away. I don't feel that doubt or fear anymore. This is it. This is the time."
"I cannot find him." She said as she stared up towards the wall. She placed a finger on her temple, then closed her eyes.
"He will not allow me to locate him!"
Mehinnerst waited in silence. Not completely surprised that Ackley would have hid himself from her, and any other mages like her. She scoured over the cites, the roads and forests, possessing the birds flying above it and the people going about their daily

rituals. She moved at incredible speed viewing, hearing and feeling everything anything living could, passing like a spirit through everything alive. She entered the forest but suddenly she saw a tiger roar, its teeth and claws bared. The stunningly ferocious creature swiped at her with its huge paw which knocked her back to the floor. Mehinnerst rushed over to pick her up.
"Wow, he really is powerful! He has done a spell to protect himself from others entering his mind, and even those of the creatures around him." She explained, as the wizard lifted her back onto her feet.
"So, can you locate him?" Mehinnerst asked.
"Well Yes and no, he is where you predicted he was. A few miles north of the eastern road, but he may move. I can't locate him again in case he...well." She touched Mehinnerst's temple with her finger and he saw the tiger swipe which made him rush backwards until he clutched the stone wall.
Mehinnerst laughed. "Don't do that again. Please just explain it to me next time."
Francine twisted her head to the side in confusion.
"In words!" Mehinnerst stated, as he stood up and brushed himself down.
"We will leave in a couple of hours. I'm taking 9 with us, and going to request some soldiers." He commented as he walked towards the door.
"Are you coming?" He asked before leaving.
She smiled. "Ofcourse!" Francine replied, and she began preparing for the journey.

Kawmdo was sitting in the prison carriage as it journeyed through the city to Blairack. The rain was pouring down, the carriage bumped over the cobbled streets rocking the prisoners inside, and Lacertian's threw rocks at them as they passed by. He pulled at his chains, feeling the cold metal on his skin.
"Look at what they've done to you!" Said a woman's voice from in front of him.
Kawmdo looked up and saw the witch that had been in his prison cell at Gila Castle.
Her black hair was soaked through and stuck to her face. She smiled wildly at him as the rain cascaded down on them.
The Lizard stayed still and silent.
"I know what you're trying to do." He thought in his head.
"What's that?" She smiled and leaned forward suddenly, which jolted the reptilian and made him recoil. He stood up which made the other prisoners all stare in disgust at his disobedience with hateful eyes.
"You see! You see how sycophantic they are! Here it is this system that is literally murdering them and they do nothing! And you want to be a part of this? This is who you are loyal to!" She shouted.
"I'm loyal to myself." He replied, suddenly thinking about how he could rectify the situation. How could he explain it? He didn't want to repeat that the witch was haunting him to another guard. They may grow suspicious of him and have him executed, or tortured.
"Tortured! Exactly! They are literally torturing you right now, albeit in a less upfront way! Look at these chains

Kawmdo! Look at these fucking freaks they have you surrounded by! These slaves that are loyal to a system and society that hates them!"
"Shut up!" He shouted, just as the fat prison guard had stopped the carriage, came to the door and scolded "What's going on here?"
Furious, the guard, jangling his keys, began opening the carriage.
"They will show you no mercy Kawmdo, but I will!" Said the witch and she moved closer to him, embracing him. He looked down at her and for a moment he believed her.
The fat guard pounded down the carriage towards Kawmdo rocking it from side to side as he approached, sword in hand. It was strange. For the first time in his life he despaired. He didn't show it of course because he had been raised to be extremely stoic, but he just stood there waiting for the blow, however, the witch gripped his arms, wrapping her white fingers with sharp black nails around them, and lifted them as the sword came crashing towards him. The guard's sword hit the chains instead, buckling them and Kawmdo fell back into his seat as the chains fell apart around him, clashing against the ground. With no time to think, he instinctively reacted, he didn't hesitate. He just jumped right back up and kicked the guard hard in the stomach which winded him and he fell back on to some other prisoners who all began shouting and cursing. Most were angry which just made Kawmdo laugh at how pathetic they were. The witch was right.

"Curse this!" He said, and he picked up the guard's sword and began piercing him with it. He roared as he did it. Hacking away. Enraged, his soul engulfed in flame. Everything that had been building up inside of him was released in a moment of pure ferocity. His whole life of servitude flashed before his eyes. All the tyranny, all the abuse. Suddenly he hated Lacertia. He hated King Gila. He hated the Overlord. He hated everything.
He began slitting the throats of the prisoners who were scorning him until the rest went quiet. He saw a crowd beginning to gather and he scraped the sword along the bars causing sparks to fly as he paced out of the carriage to face the other guard. The guard attacked, but in one swift motion Kawmdo parried the sword away and then decapitated him.
The crowd began hurling abuse. Some of the males began pulling out swords of their own. The witch appeared again and she told him to follow her.
"Please!" She begged as she saw the rage in his eyes getting ready to attack the rest of the sycophantic crowd.
"Kawmdo, please." She finally said calmly, with her soft skin gripping his hand. He looked at her, and then began to follow her as she began running.

Waendel was the only prison in Verrenum. There wasn't much crime because King Mindsley was such a democratic leader. Most of the people lived great lives. It was a very fair society and so crime couldn't

really be justified, but Hoodrow, the young orc soldier was trapped within its walls.
He had been charged with unnecessary violence having pulled a knife on another soldier he was fighting. It was lawful to fight but not to cheat which is what the little orc had done by using a blade. He still had two years left to serve when the Mage Mehinnerst came to visit him. The cell door opened and the wizard asked the orc if he could enter, knowing that even though he was in a prison cell, it was still his home.
"I have an offer for you." The wizard said.
"Come in." Hoodrow replied who was sitting down, resting his form against the old stone walls.
The Wizard entered and sat on a rock protruding from the wall.
"I'm putting together a team to enter the borderlands. We are searching for a wizard named Ackley who will be our guide. First we need to find him and then we are headed to the war at Ventricala. Because the mission is so dangerous, we need soldiers that are more expendable, which is why I'm offering 20 of you in Waendel a chance at redemption. Your sentence will immediately expire if you choose to take it." Mehinnerst said.
Hoodrow smiled and stood up.
"When do we leave?" He asked, jumping at the chance to get out of prison.
"Right now, we have your gear ready. The rest are waiting outside the prison walls for us." Mehinnerst said.

The orc followed the wizard through the prison wings to a waiting room, and saw his Verrenum army uniform waiting. He picked up his sword and swung it from side to side.
"I missed this." He turned and said to the wizard who was smiling.
"I shouldn't have cursed up! What a waste!" The little orc said.
"Maybe, or maybe it was the infinite teaching you who you are meant to be. There's a saying, young orc. When you get what you want, that's the infinite's direction and when you don't get what you want, that's the infinite's protection. Times in places like this are never a waste if you learn from it." Mehinnerst said.
"Well I certainly learnt from it." Said Hoodrow as he put on his uniform and followed Mehinnerst out of the prison where the other 19 soldiers were waiting. They were a mixture of the different breeds. Most of them were men, some were orcs but there was also a bisonite, a bull-like creature with thick brown fur and two scrofa; huge fat pigs that were known for their philosophy of pure selfishness and greed.
There were 9 mages also. 8 of them were fierce looking wizards like Mehinnerst who stood next to the witch Francine who was swaying side to side with her eyes rolled back in her head revealing only white, obviously projecting herself to another place.
Hoodrow got in line and stood with the others as Mehinnerst began to speak.
"You have all been chosen because you are more expendable than the other soldiers. You've all broken

the laws of Verrenum but have been offered redemption in replace of your sentences for accepting this mission. We are travelling up the main road North and then into the borderlands. We are searching for the Wizard Ackley, a recluse who dwells there. Ackley hasn't broken any laws and our intelligence tells us that he is peaceful, but he is still to be considered highly dangerous and a master trickster. He may not be civil with us! We have good reason to enter the borderlands to find this wizard, and so far neither myself or any of my other mages have been warned against it. We are doing this for Verrenum and the land will allow us to pass through the forests safely as long as it is in the land's interest, which myself as well as the King's top advisors believe it to be. Trust the infinite, but also trust yourselves and those around you. We are a unit and have a much better chance at survival if we stick together. If any of you break the one law and insult or attack another member of the group I will execute you on the spot. My mages will fly ahead on the road as scouts and guide us from the sky. Me and my Rookess; Francine will ride with you. It should take us about a week to reach the crossroads, from there it is a days travel east to where we will enter the forest."
Mehinnerst got onto his horse, and the rest followed. Suddenly a black horse was breathing next to Hoodrow. He turned and stroked its neck. He spoke to it in the ancient language and then climbed on top of it, and then the troop set off on their journey to find the wizard Ackley.

Kawmdo had followed the Verrenum witch to an alleyway where she rushed through an old wooden door, and ghostly passed through to the other side. The reptilian barged right into it, snapping the lock and breaking through to the other side as well. The door immediately slammed shut again once he was inside. It had been built on a slant and Kawmdo wondered whether this was on purpose.
The light shone through gaps at the top of the walls which illuminated the room, and Kawmdo began peering at all of the weapons hanging on the wall that surrounded them. There were axes and swords, and great spears all around. The place was obviously a blacksmiths. Some kind of weapon factory as well though.
"What is this place?" He asked the witch who had appeared again crawling along the outer wall in her spider-like way.
"It's where the rebels are preparing the revolution." The witch said.
Shocked by this, the Lacertian turned and stared at her.
"What do you mean?" He asked.
"There are many in Lacertia that share your dismay at the current tyranny. King Gila and his knights have tortured too many. He has unstabilized the kingdom with his wrath. Too many live in fear. He has caused them to lose hope. Everyday the people go about their daily business but in constant dread of what may

happen to them. It's no way to live." The witch answered.
Kawmdo stroked the metal on an axe that was hanging from the wall.
"Who are you?" He asked.
"My name is Francine. I'm a witch from Verrenum. I'm here to help you." She answered.
"Why? What's in it for you?" The Lacertian asked.
"I'm doing it because I love Verrenum. I'm helping you because we share the same enemy - King Gila!" Francine answered.
"I don't understand." Kawmdo replied, not understanding her love for the land and not simply herself.
"Is King Mindsley paying you?" He asked.
"Well yes, but that's not my motivation. I love the land. And Lacertia, or atleast King Gila, is a huge threat to it and our way of life." She answered.
Kawmdo continued walking around the room and staring at the array of weapons on the wall, but he was interrupted when an old Lacertian entered the room from another door. Hissing as he saw the intruder he turned right back around calling out to others who all rushed down. Kawmdo tensed up as he heard the many footsteps running down the stairs. He looked at Francine who replied, "Don't worry."
The room began filling with Lacertians, surrounding him. They all wore black or like chameleons had turned their scales the darkest of colours they could. Nearly all of them were armed, apart from one who

had a camouflage of dark blue and black scales all around his neck and back of his head.
Kawmdo gripped his sword out of instinct. The black and blue scaled Lacertian stepped forward, then he stretched his arms and put his hands out to stop the others from attacking. He looked curiously at Kawmdo, and then at Francine who suddenly appeared to the others also.
The Lacertian smiled. "Welcome Kawmdo. You are safe now, well safer! The Knights could barge in and attack us all at any minute!" He said.
The others laughed. One said "I wish they would try!"
The lead Lacertian stepped forward, "I see you have met the witch Francine from Verrenum. She has been a great ally to our cause."
"What cause? What is this place? And who are you?" Kawmdo asked, putting his sword away.
"Ah, some great questions. King Gila would not have told you of us. He tries his best to keep our rebellion hidden. He only tells the soldiers that he trains especially to contain us. If he were to reveal how many of his people were against him publicly he would appear a weaker leader, which is not something he will admit." The Lacertian said, gesturing to Kawmdo to follow him up the stairs. He moved in a strange way that Kawmdo had never seen before, just like the witch Francine. It was almost ballet-like.The rest of the rebels began to leave the room, returning up the stairs. Kawmdo looked at Francine and then followed the Lacertian.

"My name is Anarko. We have no leader here but I am the most powerful. Like Francine I am a mage. That's how I know your name and your story. Many of us Lacertians in the city have begun rebelling. They don't report on it you see, they try their best to hide the fact the people want a new way. A new law. The one law. These brutal tactics of the false king must end. Torture is wrong. His evil is wrong. The people are tired of living in fear."
Kawmdo followed Anarko up the thick wooden stairs and into a grand hall where there were even more Lacertians dressed in black and dark camouflage, some had even painted their faces.
"There is a better way. That's why we have rebelled. Do you know of the one law?" Anarko asked.
"Yes. It originated in Verrenum. Kill all who murder." Kawmdo replied.
"Yes, but there are extensions to it also, such as you must kill as swiftly as possible to justly rid the world of the murderer. If we followed this law then torture would cease to exist, as would all forms of abuse. It's the right way. We all believe in it. We are all ready to die and be tortured for this cause. We know it to be noble and just. It is the only way to see paradise. To send murderers as swiftly as possible to Danmur. Murderers like King Gila, and anyone attached to his centipede."

Danmur: The place of the worst eternal enslavement after death.

"Come. If you will. Sit with us. Please." Anarko suggested as he led them to a small circle of Lacertians sitting down.
"We have orchestrated many attacks on the knights, and pawns, and a few other loyalists to Gila, but we need more support from the people. We need more soldiers for our cause. With you, if you will join us, it would be a great bonus to the revolution. When the people find out how high up you were, king Gila's rook, second in command of all Lacertia, on our side! The great military tactician, the great and fierce torturer Kawmdo, now with us and believing in the one law. Your story and leadership would be great for us, if you believe in our cause that is."
"I don't know what I believe in anymore." Kawmdo replied, "It's like my beliefs that were once carved in stone have just been completely shattered over the past few days." He looked around at the revolutionaries who's eyes were fixed on him and nodded their heads in sympathy.
"Regardless of whether you choose to join us or not. You are safe now. If anything, at least safe from imprisonment and torture." Anarko said.

Hoodrow watched in wonderment as all sorts of people and creatures of Verrenum passed by the troop as they ventured up the Northern Road. He was kind of mesmerised by it all. It was the width of a field with the forests of the borderlands on either side. Verrenum didn't allow trees to grow on the road. The land was as alive as he was. It kept the surface even

so that the creatures could come and go with ease, back and forth from the Southern city. If a carriage got stuck, the ground would shift or dry up. Suddenly thick shrubbery for the horses would grow in front of them when travellers stopped, or water would appear as if from nowhere creating puddles for the livestock and dogs to drink from.
He watched the people pass and smiled at how amazing it all was. So much better than his old prison cell, or maybe better isn't the right word, different! It was so much different to his prison cell. All the colours and variety of faces and creatures. It was really beautiful, really something special.
Occasionally people selling things would approach them but Mehinnerst would wave them off. There were some villages every now and then, but very rarely. At points along the road the borderlands would open up a bit just enough so that people knew they were permitted to build there. Small enclaves hidden just inside the border of the forest. The orc even got to see a dragon. The biggest one he had ever seen pace past him carrying goods for its owner. It was huge and green and when it stepped it felt like it shook the ground.
At night the group would stop and rest, Mehinnerst would ask the trees to move in the ancient tongue so that they could pitch their tents just out of the way of the road and the land would comply. The trees would uproot and move. Metres of land shifted for them. Then he would take small pieces of cloth from his pocket, drop them onto the ground only for the

material to unfold and expand into tents. It was amazing to watch for Hoodrow who knew pretty much nothing of magic or spells.
At night he would watch the sky, warmed by the fires and think about how amazing the infinite who created it all was. They were like the perfect artist.

"How are your travels going?" Mehinnerst asked Francine as her white eyes rolled forward and he could see her pupils again.
She stared into the fire in front of them, waved her hands softly and began shaping it. The flames took on forms of the things she was describing as she spoke to Mehinnerst who listened intently and seemed hypnotised by the fire's movements, and her own.
"I have led the Rook Kawmdo from prison into the hands of the rebels. Anarko, the revolutionary leader, for lack of a better term, has befriended him and will teach him the ways of the revolution over there." She explained.
"Do you think it will work?" Mehinnerst asked.
"What? The revolution? Eventually, yes but it could take years. They need a lot more support to overthrow King Gila. He is not to be underestimated by any means. Neither are his mages." Francine answered.
The fire began showing Lacertians and other creatures being tortured by King Gila and his henchmen, and Francine had a rare look of seriousness on her face.

"I'll never understand why the infinite allows such things to exist." Said Francine as she let go of the fire and it returned to normal flames.
"I really hate him. I hate all their kind. I wish we could just rid them all from existence." She stated with conviction.
"Maybe we will someday." Mehinnerst replied.
"If we could just create a weapon like the sun, and throw it at their land. There must be a way. There must be a way to harness such power." Francine said, fascinated by the fire and the way it burned.

The streets were dead quiet in Lacertia, apart from the rain pounding the rooftops and cobblestone roads creating a cacophony of beats like tiny drums. The sky was a dark shade of grey and clouds of white fog blurred the landscape.
Anarko and a group of revolutionaries stopped on one side of the street. They rested against a wall, crossbows and swords in their hands. The ones who could change the colour of their scales did so to the colour of the wall almost completely disappearing. Anarko signalled to Kawmdo who was leading the other group on the opposite side to stop also. There they hid as the clacks of horses got closer. Anarko knew this was part of King Gila's Knight's patrol route. As the knights passed, the crossbows fired a bombardment of arrows and three of the knights were killed instantly, falling off their horses and carriage. The surviving knight who had fallen off his horse got to his feet just as Kawmdo came out from the

shadows to cut him down. With two swift swipes of his sword Kawmdo killed the knight.
The revolutionaries broke down the carriage door and started taking their weapons, their armour and everything else inside of value. Anarko kept picking up and putting more and more weapons in his inside pocket then smiled at Kawmdo who looked on in astonishment at the wizard's trickery. He took a Lacertian Knight chest plate and made it disappear into his coat. "You two, take the horses to our stable nearby." Anarko ordered.
They complied and led the horses away. The revolutionaries then disappeared into the night, living like insects or vermin, adapting to the constant impending peril of being caught by the torturous King Gila and his soldiers. Fear. They all felt it, and it had become like a drug to them that made them run faster, fight harder and think deeper.

A week had passed in Verrenum, and Mehinnerst had led the troop up the Northern road, across the crossroads and then a few miles along the eastern road. He stopped them all on the edge of the forest as Francine signalled to him that this was close to where the tiger had taken a swipe at her.
The wizard got off his horse and ordered the others to do the same. He spoke in the ancient language to his horse telling it to return to the Southern city, and they all watched in amazement as the fantastic creatures lined up and began their journey back home.

"I'm not going in there." One of the soldiers commented, "It's not safe!"
"Would you rather be in prison?" Mehinnerst asked.
"No, but I can't do this. We'll all die if we leave the road." The soldier replied, throwing his sword down in the grass.
Francine began laughing, but Mehinnerst was not amused. One of the horses turned around and came back, near to where the soldier was standing. The wizard moved his hand and the straps on the animal began extending and shooting out around the soldier until he was completely tied up and dragged onto the back of it. Francine was still laughing in her wild and beautiful way as the horse rejoined the others and began taking the soldier back to Waendel to serve the rest of his time.
"Look if any of you would rather be in prison, just go. This mission is dangerous but it is for the King and it is for all of Verrenum." Mehinnerst said, shrugging at the rest of them, but none of them spoke up.
Suddenly lines of smoke began hitting the ground near the troops and the other wizards began appearing. Their power made Hoodrow nervous, but he trusted them. He knew they were good beings, being that they were from Verrenum, and despite the fact they could snap his neck with one movement of their fingers, he knew they wouldn't as long as he stuck to the one law and didn't offend any of them.
"Don't offend the land. Be as respectful as possible. There are dangerous creatures in the borderlands but we should be safe. Trust the infinite." Mehinnerst

shouted, and he led the way into the forest, away from the road where Verrenum had carved safe passage.

The forest was alive. The ground moved beneath their feet at times. Swarms of insects would creep past them, clicking and snapping, given free reign by the land. Hoodrow and the other soldiers had never seen anything like it. It was beautiful, and yet terrifying. The trees moved. They heard the bark creak and crack as the oaks got into defensive positions fully aware of the wizards and soldiers that moved past them. Mehinnerst was enthralled by it all. The nature of the place. It was like being in a dream. One moment it was light and the next the trees blocked out most of the sun and they were shadowed in darkness. The land haunted them. It was there but they couldn't see it. It kept a constant watch of them. It entered their minds and knew all of their intentions. It was the parent to them all. Verrenum at its wildest.
The branches and plants reached out for them, groping the travellers as they passed, reading their minds with every touch and sending all the information to the soul beneath and above the ground. They could all feel the eyes of the infinite on them. They could all feel the embrace of Verrenum on their skin and penetrating to their cores. It was like nothing any of them had ever felt before. Terrifying and yet soothing, as if being carried on a tidal wave.

Kawmdo was standing on a beautifully carved stone balcony, watching a dragon flying in the sky. The giant

red beast looked as if it was dancing with the pink clouds, swirling around them, falling and then rising again. The lacertian was enthralled by its movements and majesty.
"I wish I had wings sometimes." He commented to Francine noticing her presence behind him.
"Yes, so do I." The witch replied.
"I've been training them today." Kawmdo said, turning to her, "Teaching them how to use their swords in the most efficient way. It's the one thing I was always really good at." He lifted his sword and stared at it. The Lacertian then turned back to stare at the dragon in the sky that was still spinning around the clouds, diving and then rising again. Kawmdo felt blessed to be alive and able to see such things.
"Thank you for saving me." He said to Francine who's eyes moved to the dragon, and she stayed with him awhile.

The sun was shining through the trees. Rays of light touched the ground as the troop were walking through the borderlands. Mehinnerst and the other wizards led the way, occasionally turning into smoke and latching high up onto the branches in the trees, peering out into the wilderness.They were still in jungleish terrain, carving a path through the land. The plants and trees, even the ground, were wild and dangerous.
One of the soldiers stopped by a tree and picked off some of the fruit it bore, only to be suddenly pierced by its sharp branches and dragged completely underground in what seemed like milliseconds.

Mehinnerst attempted to get there in time but it was too late, the tree and the soldier had disappeared, leaving behind a small dent in the mud. This caused two more of the soldiers to run off, overwhelmed by their fear, back to the road and on to the Verrenum prison.
"For fuck sake!" The wizard exclaimed, "Look troop, respect the land, don't touch anything! You have enough rations to last the journey. If you see something then call to one of us to handle it."
Mehinnerst turned to smoke and speeded to the front of the group. He led them out of the jungle and into the tall pine forests where they were all amazed by the millions of butterflies nesting there, fluttering all around them as if they were in a colourful snowglobe. After the troop had journeyed through the pine forests they came back to more average woodland. The trees were further apart and just as they got to the other side of a hillock they saw a home, carved out of an enormous fallen tree. There was moss, an array of colourful flowers, and long reaching vines hanging from the roof of it with a wild garden at the front with all different types of berries and fruits growing.
Mehinnerst signalled with his hand for them all to stay low, as he had noticed tiny, strange creatures moving around in the garden. He was about to move forward when he sensed something creeping up to his side sending chills down his spine. He felt in danger as he began hearing a low growl which is when he saw a huge white wolf slowly approaching him like a predator on his left side. Its nose was all creased up in

aggression and it was bearing its huge white teeth, like knives, they were long enough to rip him apart.
"Easy now dog." He said calmly to the animal and tried to stay non threatening as it moved closer, ready to attack if he did. It came close to the wizard as his fingers wrapped around his sword, then stopped and a gnome appeared on its back clinging to its fur. A tiny fat old man with a grey beard.
"What do you want?" The gnome said, and suddenly the group realised they were surrounded. There were gnomes everywhere, even in the trees and all were pointing tiny weapons at them.
Ludlow, one of the soldiers, began laughing, which made the gnomes laugh and turn their heads to one another, until one fired an arrow that hit the soldier, split apart as it did and in shots of colourful blues wrapped him up in a cocoon like a Caterpillar.
The soldiers and wizards pulled out their weapons.
"He's still alive! But don't take our size as weakness." Shouted the gnome who had fired the shot. Their voices were high pitched and squeaky.
"Yeah!" A few of the other gnomes squeakely shouted while aiming their ingenious weapons.
"We may not know magic in your ways, wizard, but we know it in ours! We have had to become masterminds with the way because of our size. It is how we have evolved." Said the gnome on the wolf's back. He jumped down and taking small steps approached the wizard Mehinnerst.

"Francine, check that soldier and make sure he is still alive." Mehinnerst ordered, staring aggressively at the gnomes.
"Now, what do you want?" Asked the gnome again.
"We are looking for a wizard named Ackley." Mehinnerst answered.
"Ackley! They're looking for Ackley!" Muttered the other gnomes.
"Why?" The gnome asked.
"It's no business of yours." Mehinnerst answered.
"It is when you are in our domain!" The gnome replied.
"Yeah!" The others shouted, "You're in our domain!"
Mehinnerst looked around at the gnomes all around them in the trees and then to one of his wizards. He turned back to the gnome.
"We have a request for him from King Mindsley." Mehinnerst said.
"Aah King Mindsley, of the otherlands." The gnome replied.
"Excuse me, the otherlands?" Enquired the wizard.
"Yes, yes, the otherlands, it's what we call where Verrenum has allowed creatures like you to live." The gnome scratched his chin and then continued. "And this request by the king, it is a positive thing?"
"Yes, yes, is it a positive thing?" The other gnomes shouted, keeping their aim on the wizards and soldiers.
Francine returned to Mehinnerst.
"He's fine." She said, "Just paralysed in that cocoon having strange dreams of flying." She began laughing.

Mehinnerst turned back to the lead gnome who was staring up at him stubbornly.
"Yes, the King has an offer for him, that's all." Mehinnerst answered.
"So he isn't in any kind of trouble?" The gnome asked.
"No." Mehinnerst replied, shaking his head, "From what we know he changed and has stayed away from trouble."
The gnome, being wise enough to be able to read creatures better than most of the others in Verrenum, could tell the wizard wasn't lying. He looked around to the gnomes in the trees and they all began lowering their weapons, and so the troop did the same, relaxing the tensions.
"This is the wizard Ackley's home, but he isn't here." The Gnome said, "My name is Dosigene. I am the leader. Come, but follow my path exactly."
Mehinnerst signalled to the others to follow and they did but three and then four of the soldiers and one of the wizards were suddenly launched up into the air by traps. Vines and ropes wrapped around them and hung them upside down like bats from a cave.
"Follow my path exactly!" Dosigene turned and repeated to Mehinnerst.
"Stay in single file and follow the being in front of you, exactly!" Mehinnerst ordered.
Francine turned to smoke and appeared in front of the wizard who had been caught in the trap smiling at him. She held onto a tree next to him, and pulling a blade from inside her dress cut him free. She did the same with the other soldiers, teleporting from tree

branch to tree branch, releasing them and then ordering them to carry their cocooned comrade with them while laughing as she always did, even in the most "inappropriate" circumstances.
Nobody knew why the witch laughed so much. Some said she was crazy and heard voices, others claimed she had brain damage, but the truth was, she just found nearly everything funny and knew not to take life too seriously.
She never cried, she only ever laughed. What's so crazy about that? She used to think when others would judge her for it. It seemed more crazy to her to be crying and whining about everything all the time, which is what a lot of humans did in the cities. They were like big babies trying to control the rivers of existence, and by complaining were insulting the infinite's judgement who was eternally more intelligent than those it had created. The witch Francine, preferred to just enjoy the ride.
The gnomes began climbing out of the trees and went back to work in their garden. They moved around carrying pots and watering plants and picking berries. Some dug up the soil and collected vegetables clearly enjoying the tricks of the earth by the looks of glee on their faces. It was quite a sight, thought Hoodrow as he followed the rest around the back of the house where there was a large area of grass and piles of logs all around.
"Do you see the river?" Dosigene asked, pointing to the horizon.

"No." Mehinnerst answered, peering ahead and trying to focus his view but still he couldn't see it. His eyes were not as evolved as the gnomes.
"Find the river." He said to one of his wizards who shot off in smoke towards where the gnome had pointed.
"He took the river to the eastern city about a week ago. He goes every now and then to collect some of civilization's comforts. Trading our inventions and the potions he makes from the forest. Speaking of trading." The gnome said, and turned to all the wizards and soldiers, "If you have anything you wish to trade with us then feel free to make us offers."
"I want one of the cocoon things." Laughed Bonasus the bisonite.
"That can be arranged." Dosigene said, and he ordered one of his gnomes to take Bonasus around the front of the house to see what he had to trade. Some of the other soldiers followed, as did a couple of the wizards.
"How will we get our man out of that cocoon?" Mehinnerst asked the gnome.
"He'll break free in a few days." Dosigene answered, knocking on it, "Maybe a week." He added.
"Do you know when the wizard will return?" Mehinnerst asked.
Dosigene hummed before answering, "Probably a few weeks. It depends. He usually is back between four to six weeks but sometimes he stays longer. Mostly in Throwklaw."

The wizard returned from the horizon in a ray of smoke and landed next to Mehinnerst.
"It's about 3 miles that way." He said. Mehinnerst nodded and turned back to Dosigene.
"Would it be ok if we rest near here tonight and then carry on to the river tomorrow? I can give you diamonds." He enquired.
"Diamonds? We gnomes have no use for these. Spells! Spells is what we would like." Dosigene explained.
"Well I can certainly do that." Concluded the wizard.

"What's wrong Anarko?" Kawmdo asked, noticing that the Lacertian mage looked upset as he stared at the ground twirling a feather round in circles with his mind.
"One of my men was tortured today." Anarko answered quietly.
"Shit! What happened?" Kawmdo asked, as he sat down beside him.
"They just started cutting parts off him. Savages man! This whole place is savage! We call the Verrenums and the dwarves in Crownland savages but it's us! It's us in Lacertia that are the barbarians! Why would the Overlord allow us to live like this?" He asked, looking to Kawmdo for advice.
"I don't know. Maybe because the Overlord is an evil invention created by King Gila's ancestors to keep us all enslaved. When I used to torture and see others being tortured, I used to tell myself that they must have deserved it. I don't know if I believe that anymore, but I cling to the belief that everything must

happen for a reason. That your man's sacrifice will be for a greater good." Kawmdo replied.
"Yes! Yes, you're right. I have to see his sacrifice as a simple emotionless thing. Just use it as a tool for our revolution. For our dream. That one day the one law will rule this land forever." He said and put his hand on Kawmdo's shoulder, "Have you any ideas on what we could do next? Maybe with your knowledge of the castle and the inner city surrounding it you can help us..." The lacertian paused before continuing, "...plan something greater. Could we break into Blairack? Would those incarcerated join us?" He asked.
"I don't know. I don't think so. Most are so enslaved by Gila that they will never rebel and will never be free, but it's worth a try." Kawmdo smiled.

"Do any of you want to break the one law?" Bonasus asked, laughing while barely being able to hold the tiny magical gnome crossbow in his hand.
Hoodrow began laughing, as did the other soldiers. Bonasus was an intimidating looking creature. He was huge with thick brown curly hair all over him. He had a long thick face and was clearly the most physically strong there, apart from maybe the pigs who chatted amongst themselves mostly, and on occasion squabbled over their possessions.
"Come on, someone give me a reason to use this!" The bisonite joked.
"You'll get plenty opportunity to use it. We still have far to go before we even meet this wizard." Said one of the other soldiers.

The fire was cracking nicely, and spitting out bits of burning wood as they all sat around it being warmed by this ancient pastime. Hoodrow got up and walked just a short distance from the groups. Bonasus got up and followed him to where he was sitting watching the shooting stars soaring across the sky. White lines cutting through the deep blue.
"What's up little orc? Bonasus asked.
Hoodrow laughed, "Little? Are you insulting me?" And he pulled a miniature gnome crossbow from his jacket pointing it at Bonasus who laughed loudly.
"Of Course not! It would be you who was being the insulting one by being insulted for me calling you little, therefore claiming that there is something wrong with being little." Bonasus answered.
"Yeah, that's true." Hoodrow said, smiling and putting his crossbow back inside his coat.
"I just wanted to make sure you are ok." Bonasus said, "It's been quite a journey already." The bisonite sighed. They both saw flashes of memory in their minds of the soldier being pierced by the tree and dragged underneath the ground.
"He was definitely dead, wasn't he?" Hoodrow asked.
"Yes. Otherwise the wizards would have digged him out. He was pierced multiple times. Probably through the heart." Bonasus replied.
"Why did it do that to him?" Hoodrow asked.
"Food, I think. Not out of malice or evil, but survival. Plants like that can feed off the corpse of a man for years I would suspect. Not many men travel through here." The bisonite answered, staring around at the

wilderness that surrounded them, cradling them, like being in the hand of a mother dragon, its killing claws stroking them.
"I'm fine though, I just prefer my own space sometimes. Why do you ask?" Asked the little orc.
"Because we are a team, and the stronger we all are, including mentality wise, the better chance I have of living!" Laughed Bonasus.
Hoodrow began laughing too.
"Yes, Hoodrow, I am not messiah-like. I am truly a selfish beast!" Bonasus said.
"Selfishness is messiah-like." Hoodrow replied.
"Yes, that seems to be becoming the common knowledge nowadays. It's a much better world. The greedier and selfisher those are around us, the better company we keep, the better for ourselves and everyone all round." Bonasus said.
"These gnomes. They're amazing. I love this thing. I am looking forward to using it!" He continued, holding up the cocooning crossbow.
"I'll leave you to your wonderings little orc. I find fire more fascinating than stars." Bonasus said, looking up and smiling, then he returned to the group of soldiers near the fire.
He had been a boxer before the prison waendel, and a soldier, but he had lost his temper with a commanding officer and rebelled, beating up a few others in a fit of rage. Because he was a bisonite he had mitigating circumstances for his temper, but still had been sentenced to years for his crime.

Now was his time to use what he had learnt in waendel - to be as ruthless, fierce and ferocious as possible, but at the same time to be careful who he chose to take orders from, for their sake! He didn't want to repeat what had sent him to prison the first time by following a weak leader. The only reason he agreed to the mission was because of the wizard Mehinnerst and his respectful manner. If it was anyone else he probably would have just served the rest of his time. Bonasus saw the wizard for what he was - strong, truly strong, and so didn't abuse his authority. Mehinnerst wasn't weak and sadistic. He didn't feel the need to try and dominate true alphas like Bonasus. He wasn't intimidated by the bisonite, and he wasn't on a power trip.
"How is the orc?" Mehinnerst asked, appearing from the shadows.
"He's fine. Watching the stars." Bonasus answered, pointing up towards the night sky.
"They are beautiful." Mehinnerst commented, Looking up at them.
"I prefer the fire." Said Bonasus while smiling.
"Well I can see why. It's powerful. It has the ability to destroy everything in its path. Must be like looking in a mirror." Mehinnerst replied.
Bonasus laughed, nodding his head in agreement.
"Thank you for making sure he is alright. It's good for soldiers to bond during tours like this. It'll keep us all alive." Mehinnerst said, and he patted Bonasus on his huge back and returned to where the mages were sitting around their own fire, throwing spells at it and

turning it into all kinds of shapes and colours. Greens, reds, blues, even golds. Fireworks began shooting out of it but Mehinnerst put them out.
"We don't want to bring any unwanted attention." He said.
"Yes sir." said one of the wizards.

Kawmdo and Anarko were discussing their plan with Francine who watched on, circling the Lizards, always in constant motion, stretching her arms and fingers out and scratching at the air.
"I've been to Blairack a few times in my service as Rook to King Gila. The nearest army barracks is about an hour away. The nearest station where there will be knights and a few pawns is a lot closer, but we have enough men to overwhelm them at the same time. Now we do need to figure out how to handle the dragons." Kawmdo explained.
"The dragons?" Anarko asked.
"Yes, most are at Ventricala right now being used in the war but some remain and King Gila will send everything he has. That's his nature. Even if it is suicide for the riders, he'll send them one by one if it means attacking us which he is sure to do as soon as the messengers get back to him and the alarm is raised." Kawmdo said.
"What messengers?" Anarko asked.
"They could be small dragons, birds, other mages, ghosts, anything that can travel fast enough. I'm not sure what alarm system is at Blairack but it will be the best." Kawmdo answered.

"Is there any way to prevent them?" Anarko asked.
"Not really without knowing what they'll be, unless we try to prepare for all scenarios." Kawmdo answered.
"Well let's just prepare for all scenarios. We may as well go all out with this." Anarko said.
"Agreed." Kawmdo replied, "We should divide our group into three. The first group should attack the nearest station of knights. Kill them all. Take their weapons and burn the building down. The second, will have to be our best archers and mages to deal with the dragons. They'll need to guard the outside of the prison while we go inside, if we can't capture and disable their alarm system. The third group which we will lead, will attack the prison, overpower the guards and release every prisoner in there."
"Then what?" Anarko asked.
"We fucking run!" Kawmdo answered, laughing, "If the alarm is raised then Gila will send everything he has got."
"Then maybe we should have another group attack the castle as well, once Gila has sent everything he has got to Blairack." Francine said.
"No, not yet." Kawmdo replied.
"You've thought about that?" Anarko asked.
"Yes." Kawmdo answered, "I know the layout pretty well. I spent years of my life there, and I'm in the habit of exploring and mapping out my surroundings everywhere I go, but I don't think we are ready to attack the castle yet. We need more men. We need as many Lacertians as possible. After we free the

Prisoners at Blairack, our numbers may be great enough but until then I think that would be suicide."
"I know how to communicate with crows." Anarko said, "For the alarm, if they are birds. I can get them to help."
"And if it is ghosts? Or something else?" Kawmdo asked.
"We can probably conjure a few spirits of our own, and if it's mages then I'll probably be able to handle them." Anarko answered.

It was early morning and Hoodrow awoke to the sounds of birds singing in the trees. There was a coolness to the air even though the sun had risen and it dawned on him he was free, and in the borderlands. It kept hitting him, like a wave of relief, that there was no more prison time left to do, that he was free! Free to be in nature, to see the sky without bars blocking it, to see the beautiful plants and trees, and the creatures of Verrenum that weren't trapped in the rocky cave-like walls of Waendel. He had fallen asleep whilst watching the stars and slept just a short distance from the camp fires. The others were getting up and ready to leave. Fixing their gear and making sure they had all of their possessions, especially what they had traded with the gnomes.
"We are headed to the eastern city." Mehinnerst said, "We'll carve boats out of trees and let the river carry us. The gnomes said Ackley will probably be somewhere in Throwklaw."

"How are we going to find him?" One of the mages asked.
"I don't know if we will, but we should trust the infinite to lead us. If it is meant to be and in the interest of the land then we will find him there, if not, then we will come back here. The Gnomes said he stays here for most of the year and only goes into the city to get a few luxuries every now and then." Mehinnerst answered, and he began to lead the troop away from Ackley's house and the gnomes, across the fields towards the river.
The grass was tall and thick, and hard to walk through for the soldiers, especially the ones carrying the cocoon so one of the mages took it from them with one small movement of his hand and they all stared in amazement as it began carrying itself in the air just in front of the mage. The wind blew and swayed the long grass from side to side. It looked like a sea does, the way it moved in waves.
There were trees near the river that danced with the wind as it blew around them. Their branches were the longest the little orc had ever seen and Hoodrow was sure he could see faces in the bark that would disappear as the trunks turned in circles.
The mages began using their magic to send shockwaves through the trees closest to the river, smashing their bark and wood, making huge cracking noises and causing them to snap and fall. It was quite a sight, and made all of the soldiers nervous at the sight of the wizard's powers. Each mage then began shaving the wood away with simple movements of

their arms and hands, all apart from one, who had taken all of his clothes off and began having a massive shit. Mehinnerst confronted the wizard as the others stared on with open mouths. The wizard screeched at him and then ran off into the wilderness like an animal. Francine and a few others began laughing.
"Shouldn't we go after him?" One of the mages asked, concerned with his comrade.
"No, he's gone." Mehinnerst replied, "The borderlands must have driven him insane."
"We can't just leave him, naked out here in the wild!" The concerned mage exclaimed.
"Don't lie in front of me! We can leave him. We have to. The borderlands must have a use for him. The infinite is the greatest mage of them all and I don't want to disturb its plans. We have our mission. I don't want to get side tracked. He'll be fine. There is pleasure still in madness, which none but mad men know." Concluded Mehinnerst who got back to work on the tree he was cutting through.
They continued carving canoes, long enough to fit all of the soldiers in. There was complete silence apart from the swaying of grass as the wind blew, as they all tried to comprehend what had just happened. Even Mehinnerst, who was quite old and experienced, had never seen anything like it.

Anarko was in a dark room. The windows were boarded up and the only light was coming from the candles he had lit, forming what seemed to the others

to be a random formation but Anarko was creating a portal to invite spirits into the building.
The other Lacertian mages and a few others learning magic nervously watched on as he began to speak in the dead language of Lacertia. He called out, and it sounded rhythmic to the others, hypnotising and strange. He chanted, then he went silent, as a ghost appeared in the middle of the room right in front of him.
The old male Lacertian stared hatefully at Anarko who pulled out a grimoire and began to speak, "Spirit that dwells before me, I command that you do what I say in the name of the overlord." Anarko said it firmly, making the others stare intensely, some afraid, others amazed.
There was a deafening silence for a few seconds after Anarko finished speaking. The old Lacertian ghost glared at him, wide eyed and angry. It roared and rushed towards him knocking the candles over as well as Anarko.
Then the spirit was gone, or so they thought. They looked around the room but it appeared empty until one of the other Lacertians stepped forward in a trance-like state. Possessed by the old Lacertian ghost, he began to speak.
"Why should I help you?" The spirit asked Anarko, who staggered to his feet clutching his book. He looked down at the page.
"In the name of the Overlord I demand you to help me." Anarko shouted, but this just made the spirit angry and he threw Anarko against the wall. The other

Lacertians watched on, terrified by what they were seeing.
"No!" The spirit said, in a clumsy and disturbing way, like he wasn't used to the tongue he was using, and then they all shuddered as in one shift movement the possessed Lacertians neck broke and twisted to the side and his ribs poked out from under his scales. He dropped to the floor and the old Lacertian ghost was gone. Most of the other Lacertians ran out of the room terrified by what they'd witnessed, a few stayed and helped Anarko back onto his feet.
"Try again." One of the mages commented.
"Are you mad!?" Said another, "We should never have tried this."
"It's fine, feel free to leave if you want. I will finish it alone if I have to." Anarko said, bending his neck from side to side and brushing himself off. He began picking up the candles and lit them by clicking his fingers. He moved them into a different shape and then knelt before the flames and began chanting again in the rhythmically and hypnotising way, until another spirit appeared.
This one had a longer face, protruding like some kind of alligator. It was how the Lacertians looked millions of years ago before they took on their more homo sapien-like appearance. This is how Anarko and the others knew he was old, very old.
He closed the book and put it aside realizing this spirit was far too old and probably far too wise to command. By the looks of him, he was probably older than the Overlord.

"Spirit, we are seeking your help and guidance." Anarko pleaded.
"And why should I help you?" The spirit asked, seeming relaxed and unangered by their disturbance. The other Lacertians had their backs to the wall. They were absolutely terrified by the look of the ghost.
"We can trade something. The dead must want something from the living." Anarko said, bringing his eyes off the floor and into the Lacertian ghost's.
The ghost stared back, sensing Anarko's terror. He looked away and then began to speak, "There is only one thing the dead want from the living."
"What is it?" Anarko asked, intrigued by the comment.
"The one thing the dead haven't got; life!" The spirit answered.
Anarko thought about what the old Lacertian ghost meant but he couldn't grasp it, "I don't understand."
"I'll help you, if one of you allows me to possess them and live in their form for 10 years, untroubled." The spirit replied and then moved towards the corpse of the twisted Lacertian.
"It's hard to stay in those who have not invited you in. It takes a lot of energy, but if you are invited..." He said, turning and smiling at the rest who were still clinging to the wall.
"Well then it becomes a lot easier to keep them dormant until you are ready to leave." He concluded.
The other Lacertians were dead silent. Anarko stood up as the spirit approached him.

"What is it you want me to do exactly?" The spirit asked, moving closer to Anarko whose adrenaline was peaking.
"We want you to help foil an alarm, for when we free those kidnapped in the prison Blairack. King Gila..." Anarko began to answer but the ghost interrupted him.
"King? Kings! I always hated kings. They are the reason I am eternally trapped between worlds. They tortured me. The rage kept me here. You have a deal, but after I do this for you, I want one of your forms for 10 years." The spirit said.
"Yes, ofcourse." Concluded Anarko.

The troop were in their newly carved boats and effortlessly letting the currents of the waters beneath flow them east towards the city. The mages lay back resting as their boats rocked them from side to side, and the soldiers kept an eye on the shoreline and the flowing river below them.
The two pigs, the greediest and fattest of all the creatures of Verrenum were already fishing, and arguing between each other about all sorts of pointless things.
One was black, and the other was pink, but both had a mixture of spots of the opposite colour which they tried to hide with what they were wearing, or what they were holding at the time.
"I'm going to catch the most, and definitely the biggest!" Declared Mayscott, the black pig.

Immediately Bonfield the pink pig retorted, "No no no! I will capture the most fish!"
"Aha! So not the biggest!" Mayscott said, smiling smugly.
"No no no! I will capture the biggest and the most fish!" Bonfield said, as his fishing rod began to pull, making him lean forward with excitement, "See!"
He reeled in the fish, taking it in his chubby hands, banging its head against the boat which caused a thud and created a dent in the newly carved wood, and wolfing it down so fast it looked like he had swallowed it the way a crocodile does instead of chewing first.
"Why would you catch the most and the biggest fish?" Mayscott asked, clearly frustrated that Bonfield was winning in their fishing competition.
"Because I have always captured the most and the biggest fish!" Bonfield answered.
"When? This is our first time fishing!" Mayscott retorted.
"Maybe for you, but not for me. I have always been an expert at this. I fished for my home town!" Bonfield answered with a smug look on his round face.
"No you did not!" Laughed Mayscott.
Bonfield turned to him, glaring and huffing "Yes I bloody well did!" He shouted furiously, and then the pig let out a tremendous snort which made the others laugh.
"Well I fished for the King before Waendel!" Mayscott said.

Bonfield laughed loudly. "No you didn't! I fished for the king, so I would have seen you!" He replied abruptly.
"How dare you! I did!" Mayscott scorned.
"Didn't!" Bonfield replied.
"Did!" Mayscott said.
"Didn't!" Bonfield shouted.
"Did!" Mayscott shouted even louder.
Francine awoke from her trance, and began laughing.
"Didn't!" Bonfield shouted, making sure he shouted louder than Mayscott, and they went on like that until they were both screaming in each others faces which woke Mehinnerst who told them to quiet down, which they did, each whispering did and didn't quieter and quieter until Bonfield whispered it slightly louder than Mayscott who laughed "Aha! It seems I am the best pig!"
"No, I am the best pig!" And it continued.

"They're beautiful creatures aren't they?" Bonasus commented to Hoodrow in the boat they were sharing with a few others.
Hoodrow laughed, "Yeah, they are! What were they in jail for?" He asked, looking up to the huge bisonite.
"Well, they lived next door to each other in the Southern city, like this, always competing with each other constantly trying to prove who was the most superior. They got into an argument over who could eat the most food. Well, after ransacking their houses of everything they just continued. They broke into other houses, dug up the vegetables in people's allotments and gardens, burgled the butchers and

bakery and continued until they were subdued by the King's knights and taken to Waendel where they just continued arguing over everything, each obsessed with proving he was better than the other."
Bonfield, overhearing Bonasus shouted over with pride, "I threw up the most!" Which made the others laugh, even Mehinnerst.
"No, no, no you fucking didn't! I threw up the most!" Raged Mayscott. And they continued.

"What are we going to do with them?" Laughed one of the mages to Mehinnerst.
"They may seem funny now, but think about when they are arguing over who can kill the most Lacertians! This obsession with competitiveness will come in handy for all of us then." He replied.
"I will kill the most!" Mayscott declared.
"No, no, no, you won't! I will kill the most Lacertians!" Bonfield retorted.
"No, no, no!" Mayscott replied, and it continued.

The group were amazed by the wildlife that they saw, there were so many different species. The pigs kept catching the biggest and strangest looking fish. Otters swam alongside the boats, racing with the mages who moved the waters so that the boats would travel faster which the animals seemed to love.
They passed a very smartly dressed toad who was sitting in a chair, fishing from the riverbank. He lifted off his top hat and shouted "Good afternoon." to the travellers as they passed by. The river continued

taking them closer to the city. At night, the stars would come out for Hoodrow to lay back and gaze at.
"It really was a great mission." He thought, before falling asleep.

It was the late afternoon in Lacertia when the revolutionaries began getting into position around the prison Blairack. They had all travelled separately in carriages and in all manner of disguises. Kawmdo had decided it would be the best time when the guards had almost finished a full shift as they would be more tired then.
They had disguised themselves as a food delivery carriage just in time for the finals of that day's Gladiator games. Inside, the Bishop Salvator was supervising, and all the prison staff were drained and on edge because of his ruthlessness.
Kawmdo led the carriage, hiding a group of the revolutionaries with him, leading them up to the first gate, which opened and two guards came to greet them from inside. Keeping in mind how the tiger hunts, Kawmdo immediately attacked the first one, killing him swiftly and then taking the other hostage. Holding his blade against his neck, he ordered him to open the other gate as the rest of the revolutionaries from inside the carriage jumped out and began moving through the prison entrance massacring every guard they came across. They had no time to torture as King Gila did, and they believed in the one law, to kill murderers as swiftly as possible sending them to Danmur.

As soon as the first attack began the others swarmed on to Blairack and as the second gate opened hundreds rushed inside like a swarm of insects where the games were taking place in a large communal square at the front of the prison. Kawmdo executed the remaining guard at the entrance and joined the rest who were pouring inside as the final group, led by Anarko surrounded the entrance with archers and mages ready to shoot down anything that flew out or flew towards them.
Bishop Salvator watched in astonishment as from the other side of the square the revolutionaries charged in, battling with the few guards left. There was loud shouting and swords clashed. He stood up as he saw them toppled by the superior revolutionary force. The guards were few in number and completely overwhelmed, and the Bishop only had a few dozen knights with him.
"Send a crow to King Gila quickly!" He ordered one of the mages he was with but the mage fell forward as the spirit Anarko had conjured possessed him. The spirit opened the cage of crows the mage had with him and began breaking their necks. The bishop saw this and felt great fear for he had never come across a spirit before.
The knights cut the possessed mage down but the spirit began possessing them and making them kill each other. He would enter one knight and make him stab another, until the others cut him down and then he would repeat it, moving through them with ease. They gripped their heads as he entered them and

stumbled backwards, then, once the spirit had control they would attack.
Across the square from a watch tower, the guard inside jolted to attention and began sending the small dragons to Gila castle with messages that Blairack was under siege. Five of them flew out but were immediately shot down by the archers outside the prison, and then so was the guard. Arrows bombarded him and pinned him to the wall before he let out a groan and slumped over.
Salvator pulled out his sword and backed up against a wall, optimising his defence and began slaughtering the revolutionaries that were attacking him. His knights were getting killed quickly because despite the fact they were trained for battle, the spirit kept possessing them and dropping their weapons, holding them still as the revolutionaries who were proceeding relentlessly, cut them down.
Salvator moved along the outside of the square. He scorned the prisoners who had weapons but weren't doing anything, "You will be tortured for your impotence! Cowards! The Overlord sees all!" He had just finished shouting when a sword pierced his back and came out through his abdomen.
"Yes, but it's a shame you don't!" Kawmdo said, who was behind Salvator, clutching and piercing him, "You have failed your king, and now, you'll go to Danmur for it." Kawmdo whispered as he pulled out his sword and pushed the bishop to the ground. The other revolutionaries watched on as Kawmdo stood there watching him dying.

"Sir, shouldn't we follow the one law?" One of them asked, expecting Kawmdo to finish him off, but the ex rook just stood there in silence revelling in the bishop's pain. Seconds passed. He looked at the others who were all staring at him, and then in one swift motion he jumped forward and split the Bishop's head in half with his sword.
The battle had ended, the few guards left were executed and Kawmdo moved through the crowds to the centre of the square.
"Take the keys from the guards. Release every prisoner and offer them freedom if they pledge allegiance to our cause. If they refuse, kill them." Kawmdo ordered.
Some of the revolutionaries stared at each other and then to Kawmdo.
"But sir, that's not the one law, we cannot murder!" Exclaimed one of them.
"If they aren't with us then they believe in King Gila's ways of torture and abuse, therefore they are murderers and are enemies of the one law. Now go!" He shouted so all would hear him. He moved towards the few prisoners that had been taking part in the gladiator games.
"Will you join us? There is an alternative way to King Gila's madness! Join us if you are tired of your servitude. Join us if you wish to be free, without the dread of being tortured. We follow the one law, kill all who murder. Anyone who abuses another is swiftly executed." Kawmdo shouted to the prisoners who began staring at each other, suddenly illuminated by

the fact that there were other ways of living opposed to the King's dictatorship.
"Will you? Or would you rather stay his slaves?" Kawmdo asked with contempt in his voice.
"I'll join." Answered one of the prisoners, who had a huge cut down his face from the games.
"Yes, so will I." Another said, and then more joined, until they all had stepped forward and started pledging their allegiance to the revolution.
"Good." Kawmdo said, as the final revolutionaries returned from the prison wings covered in blood, having released all of the prisoners inside willing to join, and killed the rest.

Mehinnerst had led the troop down the river for days now. The cocooned soldier had started making strange noises that echoed around the vessel but was still locked inside. The exterior had changed colours and seemed to be softening, as flakes began to crumble off and thin cracks began to appear through it.
The pigs had grown tired of their arguing and now were in the competition of who could be the most silent and ignore the other for the longest.
They all held on to the rocking boats as the river moved them faster down some rapids and into a large lagoon. It must have been about a mile across, with towering cliffs surrounding it.
The wizards with their fierce eyesight saw where the river continued and began shifting the waters to propel

the boats forward but mysteriously one by one they were stopped.
The troop became alert, peering at their surroundings and gripping their weapons. Thuds began sounding on the bottom of the boats and then they would either stay completely still or move backwards. Some of them slowly spun in circles and they all began to hear the most beautiful laughter coming from the waters, and from the rocks that surrounded the outskirts of the lagoon. Then the singing began, the most beautiful singing any of them had ever heard, apart from Francine who was the only one unmoved by it.
She quickly tried to grip Mehinnerst to pull him into the sky with her but he was so mesmerized by the music that he lashed out at her, knocking her down, so she gripped the cocoon instead and shot up into the sky with it and flew up to the top of one of the cliffs watching as the dark shadows in the water began swimming towards the boats like sharks.
The mermaids began jumping out of the water, spinning and infatuating the men in the boats, doing shows for them like dolphins. One of the soldiers groaned as a mermaid disappeared under the water again, he reached out and then dived right in in complete disregard for his safety.
"Fucking idiots!" Francine scorned, and then began laughing. She watched as the mermaids either tipped the boats causing the soldiers to fall overboard or just dragged them straight off them. None of them resisted, they all went into the water willingly, with smiling, dazed looks on their faces.

"I have the most beautiful one." Muttered Mayscott.
"Who cares!" Replied Bonfield in utter infatuation with his own.
One of them jumped onto Mehinnerst's boat, splashing him. The wizard had never seen anything so stunning in all his life. He actually thought he had died and gone to paradise. He was bouncing on pink clouds during a sunrise, frolicking with her. He felt completely intoxicated by her, like he had taken the most potent love potion imaginable. It seeped out of her skin and hair and affected everything male around her.
She posed at the front of the boat for him, pushing out her breasts and curving her long tail covered in gleaming scales that reflected the light and changed to different shades of green as the rays hit its silky surface. Another came from behind the wizard, her head rising from out of the water and she began pushing, leading the boat with the others towards some caves on the sides of the cliff.
The others that were in the water began swimming after the mermaids who were enthralling them all. Playing with them, kissing them and splashing playfully at them.
Hoodrow had never tasted saliva so sweet. It was like some perfect nectar. The mermaid pulled away from him and he swam after her desperate for more. They disappeared from Francine's view underneath the cliffs.

"Shit!" She exclaimed, wanting to help but knowing she would be powerless against their numbers. There was no point in her dying as well!
The mermaid, with her light blue and pink hair that changed to different shades as she twirled it moved towards Mehinnerst. She was so Goddess-like. Her skin was the colour of white marble but soft and tender. She pushed him down and lay on top of the wizard whose eyes drifted to the roof of the cave which was covered in a natural artwork of crystals. He then looked into the mermaid's eyes who was singing along with the rest, and her eyes were so striking, so lustrous, so stunning with an array of shades of blue, like mini oceans twirling around a black hole that he passed out, completely overwhelmed by her feminine magic.

"How was the raid?" Francine asked Kawmdo as he sat alone in a room of the revolutionaries complex. She began seeing flashes of it in his mind, in a few seconds she knew everything he had felt and seen.
"It went well. We got a lot more troops and got out clean. King Gila probably hasn't even realized what's happened yet. How are things in Verrenum?" Kawmo asked.
"Not well, the fuckers have fallen into the hands of the mermaids and I have no idea how I'm going to bring them back." She answered.
"It's just the will of the way though right?" He replied.
"Yeah." She laughed, smiled and began moving around the room.

"I think you should come here." Kawmdo suggested.
"That would be difficult." Francine retorted, "I wouldn't even know how to travel safely in my actual form, to here."
"You could do it." Kawmdo said, and he stood up and walked towards her.
"I want to meet the real you." He said, attempting to brush his fingers through her hair but it passed right through it, "I want to meet the witch that saved my life."
She brushed her hand over the scales on his hard chest and he smiled ever so slightly as he felt it. Still very Lacertian in his lack of showing emotions.
"I'll try." She said, looking up to him, and feeling something deep inside her that she hadn't felt for a very long time.
"I have to go." She concluded and her form faded, leaving Kawmdo alone with his thoughts in the dark room, as he stared up to the only light that was coming through the window.

"I don't trust him, Anarko." The revolutionary said, storming from one side of the room to the other, feeling on edge. He paced back and forth, and brushed his hands around his head.
"You should have seen it, he doesn't believe in the one law, he let the bishop die slow! I'm sure he stabbed him just below the heart on purpose so that he wouldn't bleed out too fast!" The revolutionary declared.

"This is Kawmdo! He has escaped prison, killed countless guards and knights, even the Bishop Salvator, we can trust him!" Anarko replied, disbelieving the revolutionary's concerns.
"No! You should have seen it, he is too much like Gila! He's too Lacertian!" The revolutionary replied, stopping and moving closer to Anarko, "He will betray us. He is still the same."
"But he killed the Bishop right?" Anarko asked.
"Yes! But only after he realised we were all watching him." The revolutionary said, "I think he's a double agent."
"Impossible! Me and Francine would have seen it!" The mage declared, "Look, he has been around Gila for many years, he was very invested in the Overlord's way but it betrayed him. He won't go back to it, and he won't betray us."
"How do you know?" The revolutionary asked who had begun pacing the room again.
"I don't! But surely the infinite will deliver us all from this evil land. Surely it will help us overcome and rid the world of the royals and their torturous kind and savage ways, and the book of the Overlord, and all of its lies! We will win this fight! We must do! I'm sure of it." Anarko answered.
"I hope you're right." The revolutionary stated, "I really hope you are right!"

Mehinnerst was in some kind of dream. There were bright colours all over, above him and passing by him. They reached out to him and wrapped softly like silk

around the wizard's form. The mermaid was on top of him and the scenery behind her was spinning. He was in a daze. One minute he was conscious, the next he was floating through time oblivious to everything that was going on apart from the affection she was giving to him.
He was being carried through space and there were stars all around him. He was a giant, like the size of a God, bumping into the different planets. Some burst when he hit them and juices spurted out which he drank. They were heavenly, then suddenly he was back with the mermaid and sucking on her breasts as she rode on top of him, and then he was gone again, falling through clouds but enjoying it.
He felt her hands all over him, massaging his form. Then more, there were two now, kissing and touching him, giving him more of the drug that was pouring out of their pores. Days passed like this, the wizard in complete ecstasy until he awoke to the sound of one of his mages calling his name.
"Mehinnerst!"
He jolted awake and rattled the chains that were holding him, keeping him tied to the wall. He felt the cold metal on his skin and looked at the markings. They were some kind of mermaid magic that was counterbalancing his own.
He tried to burn through the chains but it wouldn't work, they heated only for a second. He tried to turn to smoke but that failed also. He pulled at them and the other soldiers looked on still amazed by the wizard's

power as he lashed against the chains, almost pulling the entire wall down, but that had markings on it too.
"Fuck!!! Where the fuck are we?" He asked the others, finally kneeling down and peering around.
"The mermaids! The fucking sirens brought us here!" One of his mages exclaimed.
Mehinnerst looked at him, and then around as he noticed there were only two wizards left and half of the soldiers he had brought.
"Where are the others?" He enquired.
The mages looked at eachother. Everyone else in the room was quiet.
"Where are the others!" He shouted.
"They're dead!" One of his mages answered, "They keep coming for us, one by one, we've been hearing screams."
Mehinnerst rattled at his chains again, pulling at them, yanking at them with tremendous force. He twisted his body and tried to stamp at them, but it was no use. He stopped and asked, "How long have we been here?"
"A few days sir. They brought you in about an hour ago." The other mage answered.
The mage was one of Mehinnerst's bishops. His name was Tristan Phaige.
"Where the fuck is Francine?" Mehinnerst asked.
"I don't know." Tristan answered.
"Did anybody see her?" Mehinnerst asked, looking around at the others but they all shook their heads. He then realised there was a dwarf in the room with them, chained to the wall. An old dwarf with grey hair and a long beard, almost as long as his body. He could only

be about four feet high, but the wizard knew of the dwarves from Crownland, a place situated just above the elvish kingdom of Verrenum where everything was smaller, but they were twice as strong.
"Angrard, this is the wizard Mehinnerst, our leader." Tristan commented, noticing the pair had seen each other.
"It's nice to make your acquaintance, young wizard, at least it would be if we weren't in such an awful place." Angrard said.
"Where are we exactly? Do you know what they've done to my men?" Mehinnerst asked.
The dwarf exhaled and then began to explain.
"The sirens have a city, this city, this is the prison of it where they keep the males of different species that they capture. They call the city Pheronia. It is just beyond the lagoon where you were seduced. Through the crystal caves, there is a beach, and just beyond the beach is Pheronia. I'm sorry to be the one to inform you of this Mehinnerst but they will have fucked your men, extracted the semen to impregnate themselves and then executed them."
"That's impossible, this is Verrenum. How would the King not know of this? I've never heard of these things." Mehinnerst replied.
"This is the borderlands, young wizard. It is a whole nother world here! It's like an ocean and we are in the deep parts. They keep their society all female. They kill the males they birth. They're murderers, young wizard. Disgusting, vile murderers!" Angrard said.
One of the soldiers began pulling at his chains as well.

"Only nine soldiers left and two mages. I'm not sure it was worth the risk!" Mehinnerst exclaimed as he sat back down and tried to call out to Francine in his mind.
"The witch will save us, won't she?" Bonasus asked, who was directly opposite the wizard.
Mehinnerst thought long before he answered.
"Yes! Francine will figure out a way to get us out of here. I have no doubt of that. How long have you been here, Angrard?" He asked.
The whole room went silent again. Angrard had a look on his face as if he didn't want to tell him.
"Four years. I think. It may be longer." The dwarf finally answered.
"Shit!" Mehinnerst said, putting his head against the wall, "Why have they kept you alive so long?"
"I don't know. Maybe because I am a dwarf. The strength we have. I'm not sure. Many have come and gone but they always bring me back after the extraction." Angrard answered.
The group began to hear footsteps coming down the corridor. They got closer, and closer and the dread in the room began to rise. Mehinnerst stood up as the door opened. Two sirens came in, but they weren't beautiful anymore. They were the most wretched looking women the wizard had ever seen. Their skin was a dark green, scabby and scaly. They had long pointed ears and noses, and their teeth were sharp and jagged like that of a beast. Their hair was matted and clung together in lumps.

"Take that one next." One ordered to the other, pointing at the mage next to Tristan.
"Fuck!" The mage exclaimed, standing up and trying to move away from them.
"Yes, fuck! Fuck is what we'll do!" One of the sirens replied.
"You! Siren! I demand to see your leader!" Mehinnerst shouted, "I am the King of Verrenum's mage. You cannot treat us this way and get away with it!"
"Oh, we can't?" Mocked the other siren, and they both began laughing and pulling the other mage out of the room in his chains who was trying to resist but couldn't use his own magic because of the mermaid's markings.
"Wait, take me instead! I am the leader!" Mehinnerst shouted.
"Take you?! Take you?! Your semen has already been extracted wizard! You need to recharge." The siren answered in an awful croaky voice. Then they laughed as they dragged the mage away.
"You fucking pieces of shit!" Mehinnerst shouted, as he began yanking at his chains again. He yelled out and then fell against the wall.
"Fuck! Francine! Where are you! I need you!"

Francine had set up a small camp on the cliff, just herself and the cocooned soldier. She had been puzzling herself for days trying to figure out what to do. It was then that it came to her.

"Nothing! I need to trust the infinite and do nothing! Hahaha so simple!" She said and relaxed, sitting by a small smokeless fire.
It was then that the cocoon began to crack, bringing the answer of what she had to do with it. There was a groaning coming from inside of it. The witch stepped back a bit and watched on in astonishment as the crack became larger, splitting the thing in half and the new soldier began to appear.
He clawed his way out of it, groaning as he did but not in a negative way, but like how a dog does when it is relaxed. His back appeared, and the witch became unusually serious as she gazed in awe at the folded wings that the soldier now had.
"Wow, how beautiful!" She whispered.
Her eyes didn't leave him as he pulled himself up and out of the cocoon, flakes of blue dust falling to the ground around him. His skin was different, it was now as black as soot, and scaled like that of an insect. The wings appeared completely black too, until the soldier opened them and the witch gazed, amazed by it all, that they were deeply black tipped but the brightest sky blue in the centre. The soldier turned and stared at her.
She began to shed tears.
"Are you ok?" She asked moving towards him slowly.
"Yeah, I think I am, just different." He answered, staring at his hands and the new skin that coated them.
"Do you remember what happened?" Francine asked.

"Yes, I was shot, then in that." He Answered, pointing to what remained of the cocoon.
"I had dreams. Long dreams, like that of a lifetime. I was flying." He said.
"You're the most beautiful thing I've ever seen." She said, wiping away her tears.
"Thank you." He replied. And he smiled at her, which made the witch laugh, and then even louder as he unfolded his wings and began to flutter above her. He flew around in circles and then landed beside her.
"Where are the others?" He asked, folding his beautiful wings again.
"They were taken, down there, by the mermaids." She said, pointing towards the cliff edge, "I've been waiting here, foolishly, or wisely trying to figure out how to save them. They have mermaid witches. And there are so many of them, but now, I think it's coming to me, now that I've stopped looking for it."

Mehinnerst sat deep in contemplation, trying to figure out how they could escape from the mermaid prison. He thought about Francine, and figured the magic markings on the chains and walls would keep her from locating them exactly, but she must know roughly where they would be because of her telepathic powers.
"Has anyone ever escaped?" The wizard asked Angrard.
"Yes, about a year ago. He was a wizard like you." Angrard answered.
"How? What did he do?" Mehinnerst asked.

"It was a few cells along. I'm not sure exactly. I heard that he used a fire spirit to cut through the chains and the wall, fought a few of the sirens and then fled into the forest." Angrard answered.
"This wizard, what was his name?" Mehinnerst asked.
"Ackley. I remember them cursing the wizard Ackley as they passed by." Angrard answered.

Francine was ready.
"How do I look?" She asked Ludlow, the soldier who had become a butterfly hybrid.
He looked at her up and down. Her hair was still jet black but now smooth and silky. Her eyelashes had grown, longer and thicker. Her lips were a passionate red and her cheeks blushed with the girliest pink. She wore a revealing top made from woven seaweed, and she had lengthened her legs.
"You look amazing." Ludlow answered, nodding his head in approval.
Francine smiled.
"I feel amazing. Just dressing like this makes me want to seduce you and murder you!" She joked.
"Ok, so you know the plan, there's only one thing for me to do. I'll see you on the other side." She said, and then she jumped off the cliff, diving deep into the water. As she hit the surface and the water surrounded her body, her legs morphed together into a tail that covered itself in green scales. Gills appeared on her neck and she began swimming across the lagoon towards the crystal cliffs. Her eyes adapted and focused and she could see clearly

through the blue lagoon. There were fish all around her, of all different colours and shapes.
"Variety really was the spice of life." She thought as she witnessed them all like a moving artwork. She twisted herself and played like a dolphin, enjoying her new form, spinning around in the waters. Her ability to create the perfect morphing spells was unmatched. This was her greatest one.
She swam through the crystal caves and towards the beach at the other side. There were other mermaids in the water now, they swam right past her, unknowing to what she really was - the greatest witch in all of Verrenum.
She came to the surface and saw them all along the shoreline, a perfect matriarchal society. There were no men. They were free from male violence. A part of her felt like joining them as she watched them fish and frolic in the sea and on the shore, but another part of her knew that women could be just as evil, abusive and violent as men. And also that she had always had great experiences with the opposite gender. Probably because she was mature and kind, and opposites don't attract.
"Maybe I could join them, maybe I should. It wouldn't be hard to make this transition from witch to mermaid permanent, just a slightly different potion." She thought as the mermaid in her began clouding her judgement and she came out of the sea walking along the hot white sands of the beach.
There were mermaids all around, she saw some kissing passionately and found herself aroused by it.

She glanced at the small huts they had on the beach and just inside the tropical forest beyond, it really was a beautiful place.
Carrying on up the beach she came to the beginning of the city which was carved from stunning white coral. There were houses on the shore and slightly into the forest but what was most curious were the houses that descended into the water. Francine looked down over the side as she walked along the main street that stretched for miles in the shape of a crescent moon and saw houses with mermaids swimming in and out underneath the water, descending down into the depths.
An old mermaid smiled at her, who was braiding her hair on a balcony. Another approached her with fresh fish for sale, then another with flowers and another with bracelets made from shells and pearls. She continued all the way along keeping an eye out for any signs that would direct her to the prison, where the others were being held.
As she was passing a group, she overheard one of them asking, "Where is the town hall of Pheronia?"
"Oh, where are you from?" Another mermaid asked.
"We are visiting from Extebus."
It must be another Mermaid city, thought Francine as she passed by, heading deeper into Pheronia.
She communicated telepathically with Ludlow as she went, telling him exactly where she was. She knew exactly where he was as well; fluttering high above the forest just beyond the city, moving up in line with her on the main road.

She came to a grand hall, where the head sirens ruled and made the political decisions regarding the city's welfare, and then she noticed it, the one place her mind could not reach. She notified Ludlow who dropped into the forest just beyond it and began carving long lines of bark off the trees.
He had become increasingly stronger having become an insect, and fast. He weaved the bark together to create long ropes that he could carry.
Francine entered the prison where there were only two guards. This puzzled her, until she realised that they were in the safety of the borderlands, they wouldn't have had many breakouts before.
"Hello sister, what are you doing here?" Asked one of the sirens, smiling and playing with her hair. She looked ravishing to the witch.
"I'm visiting from Extebus, I was really hoping I could see where you slaughter the males that would oppress us if they had the opportunity." Francine answered.
"Sorry dear, we don't allow anyone to see the prisoners until they are fucked and sacrificed." The siren replied, to which Francine threw out her arm, pushing her hand forward and manipulating the infinite. The siren was thrown backwards by her power and slammed against the wall, split and bleeding, torn apart by the force of it and fell to the floor.
The other siren tried to run but Francine, with a twist of her hand, broke the siren's neck and she tumbled down the corridor. The witch then ran down, seeing all kinds of male creatures locked up in cells and cages,

and tied to walls. She barged into the rooms where the doors were closed. In one a naked man was chained to the wall covered in marks running all down his back and buttocks from being lashed so much. He screamed and begged at her which made her instinctively laugh. She would have helped him, but she had to at least find Mehinnerst and the others first so she turned and continued until she came to the door holding her troops. She tried to smash it open but the magic rebounded and she was flung backwards, and smacked against the wall.
"Mehinnerst." She shouted.
"Francine! We're in here!" Mehinnerst shouted back, standing up and pulling on his chains, jangling them. The witch came to the door again and tried to open it, waving her fingers on the lock to manipulate the mechanism inside, but it just shocked her when she tried, and again she shifted backwards.
"I can't get in. It won't open!" She shouted. She peered around. The other prisoners were shouting and screaming from their rooms and cells. She knew she didn't have much time.
"Shut up, you fucking idiots or I won't be able to save any of you!" She screamed down the corridor but not many listened to her because of their desperation for freedom, and most continued begging for her to release them.
"Francine, it's warded with magic. You'll have to get the keys." Shouted Mehinnerst who turned and then flinched as he saw wings flap past the cell window. The other soldiers who saw it too began standing up.

"What the curse was that?" Asked one as they peered at the window, then they flinched as Ludlow who was now completely black with huge wings landed on the bars, and began wrapping rope around them.
"Hi Bonasus, Hi Mehinnerst." He said, turning his head to look at them with his fierce eyes as he tied the knots.
"Ludlow?" Mehinnerst enquired, remembering the soldier who had been cocooned.
"Yes, it's me. I changed. Now, I'd step back a bit." He said, getting ready to fly off again.
"Well, as far as you can anyway." He concluded, noticing the chains that held them.
Mehinnerst moved towards Tristan, and Bonasus moved towards the pigs, away from the window, just as they heard Francine rattling the keys and unlocking the door on their other side.
Ludlow flew off and yanked as hard as he could at the bars, cracking the wall and creating an almighty boom.
"Well, they definitely would have heard that!" Francine said, as she rushed in and began releasing the prisoners from their chains.
She came to Mehinnerst and began untying him.
"Wow, Francine, you look..."
The wizard said, staring down at her gorgeous mermaid form.
"I know." She replied, releasing him from his chains.
"What are we going to do about the others? In the other cells?" Francine asked.

"We can't save them." Mehinnerst answered, "We have an objective to complete. Finding the wizard Ackley is our only priority. If they were good men they would not have been condemned here by the infinite."
"Then what about all of us? Are we not good?" Francine asked.
"We have you!" Mehinnerst answered, "So we must be good!"
Francine smiled, "Well I'll at least leave them the keys." She stated.
Suddenly there was another mighty boom as Ludlow pulled against the bars again, the wall cracked even harder this time, and stones began to fall from it. Then he pulled at it again and the entire wall came crashing down from the building and into the forest below. Ludlow flew to the roof and took the nets in his hands that he had spun for the troop to cling on to. He dropped the bottom part of it just outside the room and fluttered above clutching it, ready to carry them to safety.
"Quick, soldiers first, and the...dwarf!" Francine said with a confused look on her face but then shrugged it off.
"Will he be able to carry us all?" Mehinnerst asked.
"I hope so! A lot of insects can carry about 50 times their own body weight." Francine answered, "He has become astonishingly strong. We should be alright, if not, I have a back up plan."
The soldiers began throwing themselves onto the net and clinging to it. One by one they leapt into it. Bonasus jumped, but the weight had hit its limit, and

Ludlow shouted down to them, "That's it. I'll drop it if there are any more."
Bonasus, hearing this, swung himself back into the room and said.
"Let the dwarf and orc go instead."
"Hoodrow, Angrard, go!" Mehinnerst ordered.
Hoodrow patted Bonasus on the shoulder as he passed and then jumped onto the net, clinging to it with all of his strength.
"Thank you, young Bisonite." Angrard commented, as he passed and leapt to safety.
Ludlow, feeling that he was at his limit, fluttered away over the forest.
"Right, what's your backup plan?" Mehinnerst asked Francine, who looked around at Bonasus, Tristan and the two pigs.
"Well, I don't think you are going to like it." She answered, and began laughing.

King Gila was in the highest room of the tallest tower of his castle, looking down upon his land out of his window when the messenger arrived.
"What news of operation roadkill, has the bishop Salvator brought me my redeemed Lacertions?" He asked, moving from the window to his throne. He caught a small lizard that was scurrying over the armrest, and began stroking it with his claws.
"No, my king." The messenger answered, who kneeled before him and put his head down, making sure to avoid eye contact and appear as submissive as possible.

"What!?" Gila exclaimed, as he popped the lizard in his hand by squeezing it. Its blood seeped through the gaps between his fingers. He stood up and threw the dead lizard out of the window.
"Then what news do you bring?" He asked.
"The revolutionaries have destroyed a knight's station, and taken over Blairack." The messenger answered quickly, feeling nervous and just wanting to get it over with.
King Gila stayed silent, enraged, he sat back down and clawed at the gold of his throne.
"Keep going!" The king ordered.
"One of our citizens, a witch who lived opposite to Blairack, said the ex Rook Kawmdo was involved. Bishop Salvator is dead, and the prisoners are either missing or killed." The messenger replied.
"Send for my council, you may leave." Gila said.
"Thank you, your majesty." concluded the messenger, and he scurried out of the room to fetch the others.

The strange looking group of mermaids shuffled down the main street. They were awkward and were trying to blend in but they weren't doing a very good job at it. Francine was at the front, followed by Mehinnerst who had transformed from the potion Francine had made and given him into a beautiful leggy blonde.
"I never knew you had blonde hair before the grey." Francine remarked.
"This isn't the time Francine!" Mehinnerst replied through gritted teeth.

"Of Course it is, we are trying to blend in. I need you feeling like a natural woman, relax a bit!" She said.
Tristan came next, walking just behind Francine, and then the two pigs Mayscott and Bonfield who were arguing over who could pretend to be the best mermaid.
"I'm a lot more convincing than you!" Mayscott said, strutting ahead and twisting his hips.
"No, I am, look!" Bonfield replied and he dived off the road and into the water where his legs morphed into a long, pink scaled tail with the tiny black spots which he tried to hide as he noticed them.
Mehinnerst, annoyed, scorned him, "Bonfield, this is not the time!" Just as two mermaids were walking past curious to the name as it was strange for a mermaid. They walked together, arms linked and kept turning around to stare at the strange looking group.
Francine, noticing this, walked to the water's edge. "Bonnie darling, we need to get back to Extebus!" She said, Widening her eyes!
"Oh right!" Bonfield replied and he climbed out, his tail morphing back into legs as he left the water.
"Let's play who can not get us all caught, the best, eh?" Francine muttered.
"Yes." The two pigs said in unison.
"I said yes first!" Mayscott whispered. And they continued.
Bonasus was at the back, struggling to walk in his new hooves that had morphed into feet in high heels.
"I should have stayed on the net!" He mumbled to himself.

They were almost at the end of the city, nearing the beach, when a harrowing voice called out from behind them.
"Francine! Witch of Verrenum! Did you really think you could escape our wrath!"
The group froze. Francine turned to Mehinnerst and said "Run along the beach and swim through the caves, the butterfly awaits with the net on the other side. He'll carry you to safety."
"What about you?" Mehinnerst enquired.
"I'll be fine, I'll turn to smoke and flee if I can't handle them, now go!"
Mehinnerst began running with the others. Francine turned around as mermaids with tridents pointed at her hesitantly moved past but stayed far away from her, weary of her powers, and chased the others.
She moved towards the Mermaid witch queen who was ghastly looking with huge tentacles coming from her face and fingers, and her siren mage sidekicks.
Her mermaid appearance disintegrated and suddenly she was in her black dress, with bleached white skin, and black lips and eyes as if fire had burnt smoke out of them and stained the skin. Some of the sirens took a step backwards as she did this.
The Mermaid witch queen stepped forward. She didn't speak. She looked enraged. She took water from the sea and began firing it at Francine who put out her hands and created a forcefield to shield herself from it, before conjuring fire and firing it back.

One of the other sirens came to Francine's side and threw a net over her but the witch just jumped to the side burning right through it, danced towards the mermaid like some demonic ballerina and tapped her on the forehead. When she did this the siren was immediately engulfed in flames. Screaming, she twisted and fell into the water, and Francine returned her concentration to the Mermaid queen.
She began retracting her fire and deceived the queen into thinking that she was winning. She let the water flow right over her until the queen stopped to see where the witch was. She was still standing, soaked. Her hair stuck to her face. In a moment she was dry again and she fired such a strong force of fire at the siren that the others jumped into the water to avoid the heat. The queen, screaming and crawling, tried to get towards the water but Francine just moved around shifting the fire to burn her away from the waters edge. The witch really fucking hated misandrists. She stopped the fire, and the Mermaid Queen cowered, covered in horrendous burns.
"Next time, stay the fuck away from my boys, bitch!" She said, and turning to smoke fired off to find the others.

Mehinnerst and the others were running down the beach being chased by the mermaids with tridents. Bonasus at the back stopped and ripped off his heels. Tired of running, he pulled his axe from under his dress and began swinging it wildly around as the tridents came to him. They jumped back weary of him,

as he was still enormous despite the fact he was in siren form. And as they retreated to avoid his wild swings with the axe, he pulled his tiny gnome crossbow out and cocooned one of them. Laughing, he fled as the tridents began crying and trying to break the cocoon holding their sister inside.
Mehinnerst rushed towards the sea, splashed through the shallows and dived in. The others followed. Their legs changed to tails and they shot through the water away from the beach and towards the caves. Francine who was in smoke form began circling just above them.
"Bonasus! Hurry!" Mehinnerst shouted as he came to the surface and saw the Bisonite still running along the beach. The wizard wanted to change, to turn into smoke but he wasn't like Francine, he had only just drank the potion, as he saw the mermaids with tridents begin to catch up and surround the bisonite soldier, so he couldn't. He heard Francine's voice inside his head telling him to swim to the net, so he turned and journeyed through the cave.
The witch shot to the beach where Bonasus was being stabbed. The mermaids were ferociously launching their tridents into him, piercing him deeply on all sides. She hit the beach like an explosion and knocked them all backwards, flinging them onto the sand and sending them smacking against the trees. She gripped Bonasus and began pulling him away but the mermaids had grown in number and were throwing tridents at her and beginning to surround her as well, as they grew in confidence alongside their

number. One of their weapons flew by her face, slicing her cheek wide open and she fell back to the ground. She put out her hand and began flinging mermaids backwards, up into the air like ragdolls but there were too many. She looked down and saw blood coming from the bisonite's nose and mouth, and his eyes weren't moving. He was just staring up into the sky. She shook him, but realising he was dead, she let him go and shot off into the sky, speeding over the waters, through the caves as the others were gripping the net Ludlow was holding for them. The butterfly lifted them out of the water, and flew them to the cliff where the others were waiting. Francine crash landed next to them, she bounced and skidded along the earth, and then passed out because she was so drained of energy. It was over.

Francine was walking through the Southern city, everyone had been lying to her. Everybody had been watching her and deceiving her so she had created a spell to go back in time to confront them. She walked up to a famous singer and began singing the lyrics to a song that hadn't been released yet that had been communicating directly to her.
"How do you know that!?" The singer asked, before running off, bewildered.
"Why are you doing this to me!" Francine screamed and then she awoke, back on the cliff edge, her body aching from the action the day before.
It was the evening. Bats flew above the witches' eyes cutting across the starry sky. She leaned up, and

looked around. Most of the others were sleeping. They had lost their mermaid forms and were back to their normal ones now. Mehinnerst had spread a poultice on her cheek, healing it and was awake, sitting alone near the cliff edge, staring at the sky. Hoodrow rushed over to Francine.
"What happened to Bonasus?" He asked.
"Bonasus!" Francine exclaimed. "He died." She continued. Mehinnerst turned his head a bit hearing the news and sighed, but he was unmoved by it. Death was just a natural part of existence. The bisonite had died for a greater cause and was probably in a better place now. The infinite was divine. It never made mistakes and Mehinnerst had accepted a long time ago that he was just a straw dog to it. A leaf being carried on a river. They all were.
Hoodrow sat down beside Francine, who looked down at her arms and dress and saw that she was still covered in his blood. Remembering that she had come across rumours of ancient spells of resurrection, and knew of a necromancer in the eastern city, she pulled a vial from her pocket and scraped some of the bisonite's blood into it.
"What are you doing? The little orc asked.
"We may be able to bring him back." Francine answered.
"You shouldn't use that kind of magic Francine." Mehinnerst commented.
"Why?" She replied and began to stand up.

"Because they return strange sometimes. Things latch onto them in Danmur, or paradise, or wherever they go." The wizard answered.
"You think he would have gone to Danmur?" She asked, stretching herself like a feline.
Mehinnerst waited before he answered. He thought of the bisonite's last actions.
"Any of us could go to Danmur." He finally answered, "We need to move on."
The wizard stood up and began waking the others. The troop collected all of their belongings and Mehinnerst led them back down to the river on the other side of the lagoon. They followed it on the riverbank for a few miles to make sure the sirens had not tracked them.
"Do you think the mermaids will follow us?" Angrard asked, as the wizard began carving a boat out of a nearby tree.
"No. They will stay close to the safety of their city. I doubt they would venture this far from it." Mehinnerst answered.
"What are your plans Angrard? We are headed to the eastern city. You are welcome to come with us and take a safer route to Crownland from there if you wish." The wizard suggested.
"It is deeply scribed on my heart, and culture, that if any being saves the life of another, then the saved shall stay with that being until the debt is repaid. I won't be leaving the witches' side, or the butterfly's until I have saved their lives the way they have saved mine." Answered the dwarf.

"Good. We could use your strength." Mehinnerst said.
"Dwarves are strong?" Hoodrow asked, as he spun his gnome crossbow around in his hand.
"Ah yes, little orc. We are from Crownland, a country above the very north of Verrenum, where everything is twice as small but also twice as fierce." The dwarf explained with zeal, and he picked up a thick log, snapping it in half.
Hoodrow smiled, and then laughed in amazement.
"We'll follow the river to the eastern city when the sun rises." Mehinnerst declared to the others, "I suggest you get some more rest before then."
Hoodrow took his bow and arrows and went off into the forest. Being the best at archery, he was well equipped to hunt. He really didn't want to eat any more fish, which was all they could catch on the river. He fancied rabbit instead.

Kawmdo walked through the hall of revolutionaries. Many of them stared at him, acting as if they had just stopped talking about him as he passed. It enraged him and he declared, "If any of you have something to say then please say it."
"You tortured the bishop!" One of them said, standing up to confront him.
"What!?" Laughed Kawmdo, "I stabbed him to death and then split his head open."
"You watched as he was dying slowly, that's torture! It's also being said that you missed his heart for a reason, so he would die a slower death. That is not the way of the one law. We have to kill all who torture,

kill all who murder as swiftly as possible to rid their filth from this earth." The revolutionary replied.
"What can I say? Old habits." Kawmdo said and he continued walking.
"Old habits will get you killed." The revolutionary commented.
Kawmdo stopped, and the tension rose in the room.
"Are you threatening me?" He asked, turning around and glaring at the revolutionaries.
"If any one of you wants to try it, then please do." He said with contempt, opening his arms. They all stayed silent. The revolutionary that confronted him sat back down. Kawmdo turned again and joined Anarko.
"I think we have enough now." Kawmdo said, seeming happy.
"To attack the castle?" Anarko asked.
"Yes." Kawmdo answered, "We have the extra force from the prison. These are hardened Lacertians. They may be thick, but they sure as hell can fight."
Anarko, slightly insulted on the prisoners behalf, confronted Kawmdo. "They're right, you've changed, you're falling back into your old ways. I don't mean offence by this, but if you don't stop acting like King Gila someone will kill you."
Kawmdo, unmoved by what the mage had said, but knowing his position, replied. "Yes, you're right. I've been around King Gila and his aristocrats for so long I still have a lot of their old habits. I'll keep your and their concerns in mind."
Anarko nodded, "So the castle?" He asked.

"Yes." Replied Kawmdo, "More revolutionaries are coming from the south to join us. King Gila will not expect us to be so bold, and I know of a secret passageway that leads right into a main hall, about halfway up the building. From there we can move up, executing one by one the highest of Lacertia, all of those who control it. Everything is commanded from there, until we reach Gila's room in the tallest tower, at the very peak of it, and kill him. From there we will be able to rule. Those below us will fall in line, especially once Gila is dead, they will have no reason to follow him. We can do this Anarko. We can actually install a better government, a new world order for all of Lacertia, and the rest of the world. We will have peace with Verrenum and the evil will end. The torture will be no more and none of us, as long as we are good will have anything to fear anymore."
Anarko smiled.

Mehinnerst led the troop down the river. The days passed on the waters and a feeling of calmness and serenity engulfed the group. It was the calm after the storm, but they were also still vigilant to not be caught by any other of the borderland's strange and exotic creatures which there were many, like the colourful snakes that hung loops from the trees asking the travellers whether they needed food and shelter, while simultaneously trying to hide the lumps of naiver beings they had consumed in their long bodies, or the monkeys that wore ancient items of humans that the Verrenum's hadn't seen in centuries, offering them

gold to trade and trying to get them to come ashore. They rushed along the riverbank of decrepit boats and swung through the trees.
The wizards kept the boats steady and in the centre of the river, as far from the North shore as the South shore. The days and nights passed without incident, and the group finally reached the Eastern city. They all felt a wave of relief at being out of the borderlands and back into civilization, as they pulled up to the harbour and stepped onto the pier. It was the night time, and the lights of the city burned on the horizon like the stars in the sky. Hoodrow, who had never been there before, was excited to see what he could find.
Mehinnerst led them off the docks and arranged for carriages to take them to Throwklaw; the place the gnomes had told him the wizard Ackley would probably be. Francine came to him, leading a horse and told him of her plans.
"I want to take Hoodrow with me, to a necromancer I know near the coast." She stated.
"To bring the bisonite back?" Mehinnerst asked.
"Yes." She replied.
Mehinnerst paused, and then, thinking of how important she was to them as a team and how she had saved all of their lives, agreed, trusting her judgement.
"Ok. Come and find us when you have him, but if he flips out or breaks the one law, I'll send him back instantly." He stated.

"Of Course! So would I!" She commented, bowing away from the wizard with her arms outstretched, smiling wildly in her untamed way.
"Hoodrow, come with me." She ordered.
The little orc climbed back out of the carriage where the others were getting in and jumped onto the back of the horse with the witch Francine.
"I'll see you soon." Mehinnerst said, and then the witch was gone, galloping into the city with Hoodrow clinging to her.
Mehinnerst jumped onto the front of the carriage, and nodded to Tristan, who was going to be driving the other one, to follow him.

The streets outside of Gila castle were always swarming with lizards. It was the very centre of the Lacertian's world as king Gila had made it so. People were always coming and going. Riding horses, boars, dragons and all kinds of exotic creatures. Carriages came and went, crowds swarmed in the squares, some looking in awe and other in terror at the horrific architecture of torture surrounding the King's domain. Kawmdo rushed through the streets with his hood up, past the wanted pictures nailed to the doors and walls, of himself, Anarko and some of the other leading revolutionaries. He was followed by many more rebels who hid themselves amongst the crowds of Lacertians going about their business. They weaved around the city's streets like a living, moving centipede. Each group followed the group in front of them, signalling to each other and making sure the chain didn't break so

that none were lost. They needed everyone to take over the castle.
Kawmdo came to a strange looking house that was on the very edge of the castle's towering walls. There was a huge gargoyle crouching just beyond it, which didn't move, apart from its eyes that trailed Kawmdo to the door. It smiled at the ex rook and Kawmdo smiled back. He opened the door and went inside. The guards that were usually posted there were already dead. He hacked at them, and then stuck his blade into one of their corpses as Anarko and the other revolutionaries began to arrive.
"Where is the passageway?" Anarko asked.
"It's through here, in the next room." Kawmdo answered, who led the way into the adjacent room where there was a huge fireplace. Kawmdo went and stood in front of it. He spoke a few words in ancient Lacertian and the fire grew, quickly burning away the structure behind it until the passageway was visible. More and more revolutionaries were entering the strange house so Kawmdo began to lead the way, rushing up the passageway bringing the centipede of rebels behind him. The tunnel went round and round, rising upwards towards one of King Gila's halls. There were many holes in the stone wall which Anarko found strange but he was concentrated on killing the King and any of the Lacertian's inside that resisted. There was a revolution to be had. This was their chance to end the horror that was the royal's reign. He got excited just thinking about it as he followed Kawmdo. No more torture. No more fear. No more Overlord and

all of his tyrannical bullshit. A new era was to be dawned.
He began to smell smoke, and looking up he saw a fire, and then saw Kawmdo jump right through the dancing flames to the other side. Anarko followed, he leapt through the flames landing in the hall on the inside of the castle, but before he could lift his head and look around he heard a gate smash down from behind him, and the rest of the revolutionaries began screaming. He turned and saw that the holes in the walls of the tunnels were shooting fire out of them. He looked on in horror as he heard the entire revolutionary centipede being burnt alive, hundreds of them all screaming at once. He took out his sword and began slashing at the gate but it did nothing but send sparks flying back at him. He tried to use his magical powers but the magic on the gate was the strongest he had ever felt, so much so that he recoiled as he felt it was venomous. He turned as he heard clapping and footsteps come towards them. He saw King Gila approaching, smiling widely, his eyes fixed on the Lacertian mage. Anarko turned and stared at Kawmdo, who paced to the side of the king. The rook didn't look back. He just looked down, and tried to empty his mind as he felt as sick as Anarko about the betrayal, but his loyalty was to Lacertia, and King Gila was the leader, ordained by the Overlord to rule. Anarko, jolted out his hand trying to attack the King with magic but King Gila kept moving forward, untouched by what Anarko could do, for the King was

also a mage, and a much more powerful one than Anarko having been chosen to be by the Overlord. Furious, Gila put out his arm and twisting his hand began dislocating the revolutionary leader's joints. Anarko fell to the floor screaming and wriving in pain.
"King Gila, please may I speak?" Kawmdo shouted out, before kneeling. In other circumstances, the king may have begun torturing him as well, but Kawmdo had done such a fantastic job, albeit with Gila's help. Their relationship stretched back to when they were children running around the castle. Gila being slightly older. He favoured Kawmdo over everyone, apart from his royal ancestors of course.
He stopped torturing Anarko and turned to the rook.
"You may." He stated.
"Please kill him quickly. Just please. I can feel the dread in him. My loyalty to you is unquestionable but I have lived side by side with this lizard for months." Kawmdo said, daring not to look up.
"Ahh Kawmdo, my finest soldier, my friend." The King replied, placing his strong hands around the rook's neck and gently guiding him to his feet. Their eyes met. Kawmdo's teeth began chattering. "I'm not as strong as you, I cannot..."
"Kawmdo." Whispered the King, "Strength comes in many forms. Go, go to your chambers. Eat. Get drunk. Fuck as many of the whores as you like. Your work here is over. Now let me handle the rest."
The pair stared at each other, and more words were communicated by their eyes than with their tongues. Kawmdo, loyalist servant to the king but attached to

the revolutionary, was despairing. He had done his duty, yes, but was cursed with more empathy than the King, who saw in Anarko his most despicable enemy, a traitor to all of Lacertia, himself and the Overlord. Kawmdo didn't have the heart to understand what was necessary.
"Go." Gila ordered, and the rook began to walk away as Anarko screamed his name. He made it easier by cursing the rook for betraying him, and Kawmdo returned to his chambers leaving Anarko behind to receive the most brutal torture King Gila had ever dished out.

Hoodrow clung to Francine as she led the horse through the streets towards the coast. The sun was shining, warming them both. They had been riding for two days now, sleeping on the horse. She whispered to it at times, in the old tongue, and it knew what she was saying to it. They came out from behind the houses and arrived on a coastal road where they could see the beach, and the dazzling silver ocean beyond it.
Just before the grass turned to sand, before the beach, there were sporadically placed cottages, and one of them was surrounded by tall dark green conifers. Francine led the horse to it and then she jumped down. Hoodrow followed as she stepped through the conifers and suddenly they were in a huge graveyard about a mile across, enormous compared to how it looked from the outside.

There were very old orcs bustling around, digging graves and carrying stones, and in the middle was an ancient church with cottages on the side of it. The pair followed the track to them. They were made of old crumbling stone and there were strange markings carved on the outside of it, as well as the oldest orc Hoodrow had ever seen, sitting reading a newspaper with crooked glasses on.
"Can you tell us where the necromancer is please?" Francine asked.
The orc looked up from beyond his glasses. It smiled, and suddenly he morphed into a beautiful woman. She began to laugh, as did Francine.
"Rennice, it's good to see you." Francine said as the two witches embraced.
"It's really good to see you too." She replied and she began stroking Francine's hair.
The two stared at each other, appreciating being in one another's company for a moment, and then they began kissing passionately. Hoodrow watched on as Rennice's hair burned from light ginger to crimson red. Francine pushed her through the door and the witches kept kissing while walking inside.
"Hoodrow, come." Francine shouted, so the orc shrugged, and followed, watching as the pair began tearing each other's clothes off. Francine, being the more dominant one, pushed Rennice down and she began licking her pussy while the witch gripped the other's hair which had darkened yet again, it was now the darkest red the little orc had ever seen.

Francine took a small vial from her pocket and passed it to Hoodrow.
"Here, drink this." She ordered, and the orc obeyed. He drank the blue liquid and suddenly began to feel more turned on than he had ever felt in his entire life. He leered at the curves of Rennice as she bent her round booty in the air, tempting him to take her from behind. The orc obliged her. He pulled his pants off and began fucking her doggystyle. He gripped at the flesh on her hips and pounded her while Francine forced her head down on her wet pink flower. The white and black witch moaned and threw her head back as her face whitened and her lips darkened. She twisted her hips and humped Rennice's face, and the fucking intensified until all three were having orgasms and Hoodrow pulled out, falling back onto the floor, moaning.
"Oh my infinite, that was amazing. You've got even better." Rennice commented.
"Yes, so have you." Francine replied, breathing heavily. Her body buzzing all over.
"So what else can I do for you?" The necromancer asked as she wiped her face down and began getting dressed.
"We lost a comrade in the borderlands, I've brought some of his blood." Francine said.
"What type of creature was he?" Rennice asked.
"A bisonite." The witch answered.
"A bisonite, interesting. And his nature?" The necromancer enquired, as she began collecting items off her mantelpiece.

"He was good." Francine answered.
"Good in the common term?" Rennice asked.
"No, well, maybe, but he was good in the way of the ancients as well." The witch answered.
"How much of the blood did you get?" Rennice asked.
"Enough." Francine replied, pulling the vial from her dress and passing it to the necromancer who looked at it, swirling it around inside the glass.
"Ok, let's do it. We'll use the church next door." Rennice concluded. She looked at Francine and sighed, "You are so good in bed!"

The carriages had arrived in Throwklaw carrying the wizards and the soldiers. Mehinnerst had split the group into pairs with orders to meet at the crooked crow, a pub and inn near the centre of the small town at sunset if they couldn't find him.
He had been along the harbour and checked every restaurant and pub along the seafront. They had checked the meeting places of witches and wizards and stumbled across an ancient library with dusty books so old they were coming apart but the wizard Ackley was nowhere to be found. Nobody seemed to have seen him or knew of him, and Mehinnerst began to wonder whether they would tell him, even if they did.
Himself and Tristan arrived at the crooked crow and booked themselves and the others a room.
"What would you like to drink?" The bar man asked.

"Erm, I'll have a bottle of deerblood." Mehinnerst answered, "Do you want anything?" He asked Tristan.
"Yeah, I'll have the same." Tristan replied.
Ludlow and Angrard entered the pub and joined the rest of the soldiers at their table. Mehinnerst took his wine and went to join them.
"Do you know of the wizard Ackley?" Tristan asked the bar man as he passed him his drink.
"Ackley?" The bar man replied, thinking. "No, I don't." He answered, shaking his head, "Sorry. Why? Is he a fugitive?" He asked.
"No, just someone King Mindsley has sent us to find." Tristan answered, "Thanks for the drink."
"You're welcome." The bar man replied, drying a glass and watching the wizard walk away.
"So, did any of you get any leads?" Mehinnerst asked, sipping on his deerblood.
"No, we did find that there is a coven gathering tonight at a holy place in the woods nearby, but apart from that, nothing." Bonfield answered.
"Well, technically it was I who discovered that." Interrupted Mayfield.
"No, no, no, it was me that discovered that!" Bonfield replied, huffing and puffing, and it continued.
"Ludlow?" Mehinnerst enquired.
"Nothing, I got a lot of stares, and a few women trying it on with me but nothing of the wizard Ackley." He answered, making the rest of the group laugh.
"What should we do sir? Will we head back into the borderlands and wait at his home?" One of the soldiers asked.

Mehinnerst paused, he thought for a few seconds, "You know what, yeah! Fuck it! We'll head back along the eastern road tonight and go back to where we found his tree house. Let's just get drunk now. Francine will be back with Hoodrow tomorrow. She has been communicating with me that she will be bringing Bonasus back as well." Concluded Mehinnerst, and the group took the night off, drinking until the early hours of the morning.
The bartender, who had been observing and getting to know them, and had gone to see the wizard Ackley, who was drinking in the back, out of the way of others, decided that they weren't a threat, so walked to their table and struck up a conversation with the group.
"What do you want with Ackley?" He asked.
Mehinnerst, realising that they had a lead, explained, and offered the bar man diamonds if he could lead him to the wizard.
"And, you're sure he isn't in any kind of trouble?" The bar man asked.
"No, it is against our ways to lie. If he was in trouble, then we could not catch him in that way without forfeiting our souls to Danmur as well. We need a guide, through the borderlands. That is all. It's just a job opportunity, if he chooses to take it. You clearly know him, how?" Mehinnerst asked.
"He is my son." The barman answered, sitting down at the table, which quieted the rest of the group.
"Can we see him? Do you know where he is?" Mehinnerst asked, "I promise you, our intentions are

to offer him a job, and that's it. He hasn't broken any of the King's laws recently! Has he?"
"I wouldn't know, I taught him not to speak of such things, even with me." The bar man replied, who finished off his own drink and then stood up.
"Ok, just you though, he says he will speak with you tomorrow, in the afternoon." He stated.
"Ok." Mehinnerst replied, standing up as well and shaking the bar man's hand, excited that things were finally going to plan.

"When will the Verrenum witch come?" King Gila asked his rook Kawmdo.
"I don't know. She appears sporadically. It should be soon though." He answered, looking around the cell and at the markings all over the walls that Gila had painted on them in order to trap her.
"I've given orders to the rook Horridum to lead for the next few days." The King said.
"I doubt it will be that long. Probably tonight or tomorrow." Kawmdo replied.
"Good. I'm looking forward to meeting this bitch." Concluded the king.

Francine and Hoodrow were sitting together on the opposite side of a huge stone slab in the ancient church. Rennice, who had been painting symbols all over it that collectively resembled the shape of a human being began to speak in the ancient tongue. She took the vial containing the blood of Bonasus, and poured it out onto the slab where the heart would

be. She continued chanting, when the blood began to shift and multiply.
After a few seconds there was a heart, and spreading from the heart other organs began to appear, as well as bone, muscle and fat. After a few minutes the skin began to grow and Hoodrow could see the beginning of Bonasus start to appear. He stood up, unused to such things and walked backwards to one of the benches in the church.
Francine watched on in amazement, engulfed by the necromancer's power and skills. The fur began to grow on Bonasus, and the eyes filled his head, until the ritual was complete.
The bisonite coughed. His eyes opened and he flinched.
"It's ok, it's me, Francine." The witch said, putting her hand on his side and stroking the thick fur.
"I went to Danmur." The bisonite despaired. He began to cry. He got up off the slab and staggered around. He then sat on one of the benches and repeated, "I went to Danmur!" He put his head in his hands.
"I can't believe it. What did I do that was so wrong?" He looked at Francine and then at Hoodrow.
"I threw away my life. Even if it was in exchange for two others. That was my sin." He realised as he stared at the orc and then back at the witch thinking of when he jumped off the net back in Pheronia.
"Never again!" He said and he began to leave the church.
"Bonasus, wait." Francine called out.

"No! Leave me alone. I need to be on my own for a bit." He exclaimed.
"Ok, but don't go past the conifers!" The witch shouted, and she turned to face Rennice.
"He went to Danmur? For that?" She asked.
"Yes, throwing your life away, even for another, is a great sin." Rennice replied as she began to clear up the items used in her ritual.
"That's..." Francine commented, but Rennice interrupted her, "the infinite! It treats us like straw dogs, no time to mess around and keep us dependent. It teaches us in brutal ways. You know this."
Francine stayed silent, in deep contemplation, then she began laughing "Fucking hell!"

Hoodrow walked through the graveyard of long green grass and crumbling stone to his friend Bonasus who was sitting on a bench staring solemnly at the ground. The bisonite was watching a worm wriggle on the stone path, desperate to live and yet being tortured by the infinite. The lowest on the food chain.
The little orc sat beside him and followed his gaze to the wriggling worm. Hoodrow picked it up and threw it onto the grass, but the bisonite's view moved to another one, and then another one.
"You can't save them all. Maybe they don't deserve to be saved. Maybe they sinned as I did, and now have been reincarnated for eternal torture, their souls passing from pathetic form to pathetic form." The Bisonite commented.

"What was Danmur like?" Hoodrow asked.
Bonasus sighed. He stared ahead in front of him as if he was in a daze.
"It was like anarchy. Torture everwhere. These horrendous creatures with unlimited powers ruling over those of us condemned there. There was fire, all over, the ground was volcanic, and ash, smoke and terror filled the air. I can't explain it, Hoodrow. There are no words in this dimension to describe it." The bisonite answered. Suddenly Bonasus turned his head and Hoodrow jolted back as he saw the most evil smile on the bisonite's face, and his eyes had turned completely black.
"What's wrong?" Bonasus asked as his eyes returned and a solemn look masked his face again.
"Nothing." Hoodrow replied.
Rennice came rushing out of the church. "Hoodrow!" She shouted. The orc turned and began running towards her. Bonasus followed.
"It's Francine." The necromancer continued, "She has disappeared! I heard her scream and then she was gone."

King Gila ordered Kawmdo to leave, which the rook did, as the most powerful mage in Lacertia held out his grasp on the Verrenum witch in front of him. Her form tried desperately to escape but she was stuck there, glued to the floor by his powers and the markings on the wall.
"What has he done!?" She asked, in regard to Kawmdo and then she suddenly saw it all flash

through King Gila's mind. How he had tricked them all from the very start. How he knew exactly how to manipulate their minds. How releasing the rook into the wild was just a way to trap the growing band of revolutionaries that were disloyal to him. She was impressed by his cunning. It was amazing. He was so powerful.

He walked towards her and she flinched as he approached. He gripped her by her arms and without saying a word entered her form, possessing her completely. Suddenly she fell onto the stone bed and she stared up at herself, Gila possessing a form of her. He walked out smiling and then slammed the cell door shut behind himself. Kawmdo, who was standing just down the corridor, turned to see Gila in the witch's form.

"Join Horridum. I have work to do." The king declared and then he disappeared, leaving only Francine shouting and banging on the cell door behind.

Kawmdo walked back to the bars and looked at the witch who became silent as he approached.

"You betrayed us!" She exclaimed.

"No! I stayed loyal to the king." He replied.

"But, I saved your life." She retorted.

"No, he just made you think you did." He said, "Goodbye Francine."

The Rook walked off and the witch turned away also, and sat down on the stone bed. She kept seeing flashes of Anarko and the others screaming and for the first time in her life she felt regret. She should never have gotten involved. She should have just stayed in the southern city and done magic, and lived a somewhat normal existence, instead of chasing the spells and propaganda of the castle. She felt as if she had deceived herself. She felt like Bonasus; like she had sinned. She must have sinned to end up like this, stuck in this prison cell in the very heart of Lacertia, forever, or to be tortured. How could she have been so foolish? The witch screamed in anger and frustration, which lit up the markings on the wall as they suppressed her powers.

"What happened to you?" Hoodrow asked as he saw Francine reappear in the church. The witch, possessed by King Gila who knew her mind completely laughed and replied, "I transferred myself too thoroughly and it gave me a shock, nothing to worry about. Come, we need to head to Throwklaw to meet up with the others." Gila stretched the witches fingers and scraped the air as she did often as he began to leave. Hoodrow and Bonasus followed and the witches said their goodbyes. Bonasus stared in awe as they french kissed. "Wow." He Commented to the little orc who laughed.
"We need to get you some new armour." Said Gila possessing Francine to Bonasus.
"I did manage to get your axe." And he reached into her dress pocket where she kept rooms full of items and pulled the axe from it, passing it to the bisonite who gripped it and smiled.

Mehinnerst was excited to finally meet the wizard Ackley but also a bit nervous, for he was quite a character and there were many rumours about him. They said he had become extremely powerful through practice of light but also dark magic. The bar man led the wizard to the back of the crooked crow where there were barns in the shape of a square. He pointed to it and said "He's at the very end one. He prefers to drink alone. I hope, for your sake you haven't lied to me because if you approach him with evil intention he'll clock onto it, as will Pyra."
Mehinnerst turned towards the bar man and asked, "Who's Pyra?"
The bar man began laughing, "His fire spirit!" He patted Mehinnerst on the back and said "Good luck." Before returning to the bar.
Mehinnerst cautiously entered the barns. He walked down towards the end one where the other wizard was meant to be. He passed a few animals and then in one of the stys he noticed a pair of corpses. He pulled out his sword in shock, and then saw Ackley appear, with his hood up, leaning against a wall. He looked at Mehinnerst, and then put his head around the wall to see what had jolted him.
"I didn't kill them. I use a spell when I stay at new places, an old protection spell. It means that if anyone comes near where I'm staying with evil intentions, they die." Ackley said, and then he turned and headed into the room he had been drinking in. "Come." He said to Mehinnerst who followed and was jolted again as he saw a small blue flame blow up into a full size

woman of fire burning with rage and aiming a bow and arrow at him. Ackley put his hand out and said "No." The fire spirit looked at him for a moment.
"He's ok." Commented Ackley, and Pyra miniaturized again into a tiny blue woman burning with flames. She flew towards Ackley and warmed him.Then she became curious of Mehinnerst. She cautiously approached him, bouncing in the air and the pair rotated around each other.
"I've never seen a fire spirit before." Mehinnerst said, still clutching his sword. He realised she may find it threatening and put it away, which made Pyra appear more friendly towards him.
"Yeah they're great. It's like having a God in your pocket." Ackley replied, who was packing his few items away into a bag.
"Where did you find her?" Mehinnerst asked, still watching her in intriguement.
The wizard Ackley saw flashes of Danmur in his mind.
"Her last owner, he was stupid enough to keep her in a small jar, like an insect or something. He kept her like a prop to show off to others. She loved him. They're very loving, very loyal, but if a being takes them for granted or harms them, they go from a warming flame to a devastating inferno in a matter of seconds." Ackley said, and as soon as he took a step towards Pyra she rushed to him and began spinning around him.
"She burnt right through the jar, set him and the entire house on fire."

"That didn't answer my question?" Mehinnerst enquired.
Ackley smiled, "I didn't want to answer your question. What do you want Mehinnerst?"
"You're a student of the old ways Ackley?" Mehinnerst asked.
"Yes, I tend not to speak unless it is necessary, and I rarely tell others what I do anymore. It's why I drink alone. It's much better that way." Ackley answered, putting the last of his items in his rucksack.
"You don't keep your items in your pocket?" Mehinnerst asked.
"Nah, I never bothered to figure out how to do that." Laughed Ackley, throwing the backpack on, "Or maybe I just prefer some things the old fashioned way. So, what is it you came for?"
"The King has an offer for you. We need a guide through the borderlands at Ventricala." Mehinnerst answered.
"Why?" Ackley asked.
"King Mindsley and the other members of the council believe that King Gila will send an army through it in order to attack Verrenum from a new angle." Mehinnerst answered.
"Nah, that's impossible. They would die. The land would swallow them." Ackley said and he began to leave the back room of the barn.
"Is it? Have you not noticed the change in the land recently? There is a shadow hanging over us. It's in the earth, the water, the people. Something different is

coming, like a new age." Mehinnerst said. Ackley stopped.
"But Verrenum is such a great country, a great people. Why would the infinite prefer Lacertia over it?" Ackley asked, turning towards the other wizard.
"You haven't been in the cities recently, Ackley. The culture is changing. The people are destroying themselves. True art, architecture, even beauty is becoming rare now. The people think they are enlightened but really, from what I've read of the civilisations of old, they're common signs of a civilisation coming to an end. I can give you spells, diamonds, a paradisian stone?" And when he mentioned the stone, Ackley suddenly showed interest.
"You have a paradisian stone?" He asked.
"Yes, King Mindsley has many at the castle." Mehinnerst answered.
"And he would give me one in exchange for guiding you through the borderlands at Ventricala?" Ackley asked.
"Yes." Mehinnerst answered.
The nomadic wizard paused. His eyes squinted slightly.
"You know what hunts me don't you?" Ackley asked.
Mehinnerst paused as well, and then looked confused, shaking his head.
"Ok, I'll do it for a paradisian stone. I don't know the borderlands at Ventricala, but they will be the same as where I live. I can guide you safely through them."
"Ok." Mehinnerst said and he shaked Ackley's hand.

"I just need to say Goodbye to my Father." He said and they walked back through the barn to the crooked crow.

Rook Kawmdo entered the room where the council was meeting, aggressive in his mannerisms as always. He found aggression helped when dealing with others, especially during the council meetings.
"Welcome back Kawmdo." Rook Horridum said, "We have orders from the King to continue with the organisation of Operation Roadkill, while he is away."
Kawmdo walked to the table where the huge map of Lacertia and Verrenum was on display.
"I'm happy to lead them if the council desires it." He said.
"We have already been discussing that, and have decided on myself for this task, as you have just come back from yours with the revolutionaries. Great job by the way!" Horridum said, and the rest of the council laughed and patted Kawmdo on the back. He smiled wryly. The rook was still feeling intensely about it. He could still hear Anarko's screams.
"We will need you to lead the council here and be the one to report our efforts to the king." Horridum commented. Kawmdo nodded, "Who are you going to take with you?" He asked.
"Just a regular battalion, and a few mages." Horridum answered.
"You should take the Anaki." Kawmdo suggested.
"For this?" Questioned Horridum.

"Yes, it's the most important mission we have ever tried. We may as well use everything we can. They are the most elite of our fighters. It's all good saving for a rainy day but what if the rain never comes? May as well use what we have while we have it." Kawmdo said.
The room went silent. The bishops looked at Horridum who was contemplating.
The Anaki. The most fierce warriors that Gila kept in their own part of the castle, excluded from every part of Lacertia apart from the King's demands. They hadn't been used in a hundred years. They were dark and mysterious lizards, dwelling inside the shadows of a nightmare. All they did was practise the art of warfare, including the study of the magical scripts apparently written by a messenger from the Overlord himself. They didn't indulge in anything other than these two artforms. They were warrior monks that had taken a vow to do nothing else.
"Yes." Agreed Horridum, having given it enough thought, "I'll take the Anaki with me."

"They need a guide, through the borderlands at Ventricala." Ackley explained to his Father in the living room above the crooked crow.
"Have you been to that part of the borderlands before?" His Father asked.
"No, but the gnomes will have. I might take Dosigene with me, if he'll come." Ackley replied, "Or atleast ask for his advice. They know the land better than me."

"I think he will, after what you did for him." His Father said.
"Yeah I think so too. They treat me as if I'm one of them now." Laughed the wizard.
"You take care, and swing by for a drink next time you're in these parts." His Father said. The pair hugged and Ackley went downstairs and out of the doors where Mehinnerst was gathering his troop. They all watched as the wizard Ackley approached. Ackley looked in awe at the many different creatures they had with them. The pigs, the butterfly, the men, the orc, a dwarf, a bisonite and the Verrenum witch Francine. He recognized her and smiled, but when she smiled back he saw the Lacertian king possessing her form. Shocked by this, he threw her against a carriage with tremendous magical force. Mehinnerst shouted, "What are you doing!?" He tried to subdue Ackley but the nomadic wizard was too powerful.
"That's not your witch Mehinnerst. It is Gila." He answered, and when Mehinnerst looked again he saw the same Lacertian face in Francine that Ackley had seen. King Gila crouching, slammed his hand on the floor and pushed his other one out in an attempt to shift the way to break their necks. The pigs fell, as did Hoodrow, Ludlow and the men. The bisonite and Angrard recoiled, as did the 3 wizards. Bonasus came back swinging his axe but Gila gripped it and in the swiftest movement the others had ever seen jumped around him and swung it into the bisonite's back which put him to the ground with a mighty thud.

Pyra became an inferno next to Ackley and began firing arrows of flame at Gila in rapid repetition, but the King jumped and dived away from them. He spoke in ancient Lacertian and suddenly Ackley began feeling sick. He shuffled backwards, watching as the other three mages and Angrard fell to the floor convulsing. Their veins popped up through the skin, as Gila pumped venom through them. Ackley resisted and pulled his sword, attacking the Lacertian King who conjured his own sword from behind his back.
The two began fighting, and Pyra joined in with a sword entirely of flame. Ackley's Father, seeing the dead wizards and soldiers from an upstairs window, and his son in combat, pulled out a crossbow, and aimed it at Gila who noticed and dropped the bar man to the floor filling him with venom.
Ackley used this distraction and pierced Francine's chest which knocked the lizard king right out of the witch and back into Lacertia. Suddenly he saw the witch was back in her form, and she despaired as he cradled her in his arms.
"I'm so sorry." He said. He looked around at the dead, and then at Pyra who was burning intensely, and he used his powers to shift time and go back to when he was walking out of the crooked crow just minutes before.
They all watched as the wizard Ackley approached. Ackley again looked in awe at the many different creatures they had with them. The pigs, the men, the butterfly, the orc, a dwarf, a bisonite and the Verrenum witch Francine.

He recognized her and smiled, and when she smiled back he saw the Lacertian king possessing her form, but this time he stayed calm and pretended he couldn't see it. He approached her and told her how fond he was of her magic.
"I've read your grimoire so many times." He said, smiling, pretending he didn't know of her possession by the Lizard king.
"Thank you." She said, smiling back wildly.
"It's nice to finally meet you, Ackley." Said Tristan, shaking the wizard's hand.
Ackley smiled and said, "Thank you."
"So, what's the plan, Mehinnerst?" He turned to the lead wizard and asked, as the others marvelled over Pyra who was loving the extra attention she was getting. None of them had ever seen a fire spirit before. They were one of the rarest creatures of Verrenum. Not many had journeyed from Danmur to the world above.

Rook Horridum walked down the corridor that led to the Anaki's quarters. He was nervous. They were very intimidating creatures, and he had never met any if them before; only heard stories and rumours of their ways.
He came to the huge, bolted door where one of them passed through it like a ghost, jolting him.
"I'm here on behalf of King Gila." Horridum declared, stepping backwards, in fear of the elite warrior.
"We cannot take orders from anyone but he who is ordained by the Overlord to lead." The Anaki replied,

in a very serpentine way. He immediately saw King Gila in his head approving of Horridum.
"Very well." The Anaki said, then he turned, opened the door and led the rook inside.
They passed through another corridor and then into the main hall where the other Anaki were training. Horridum saw them fighting in the most amazing styles of combat, some with just their fists, others with weapons. They were surrounded by weapons; they covered the walls from the bottom to the very top. They walked through the hall and onto an enormous balcony where the gargoyles of Gila castle were moving around and watching over the Anaki beneath them. Horridum had never seen them move before and was in awe of them. They were huge, crunching stone, cracking as they moved, and hideous looking creatures, built by powerful Lacertian mages centuries ago in order to protect the castle incase of invasion. The Anaki led Horridum to their leader: Valestine, who greeted Horridum, "What are our orders?" The leader asked.
They stood militantly in a circle around Horridum who answered, "The king requires a group of you to protect us as we travel through the borderlands at the Ventricala pass. We leave tomorrow. Pick the best of your lizards and join us at sunrise for departure." Valestine nodded to the rook.
Rook Horridum, still fearful, of not only the Anaki but the Gargoyles that they communed with, turned quickly away from Valestine and then left, happy to get away from their quarters.

The days passed by, and Mehinnerst led the group through and then out of the eastern city and up the eastern road back where they came from.
Dosigene the gnome, being the smartest of all the creatures in Verrenum had already predicted Ackley's wishes, and met them with a few gnomes bringing his wolf; Robin as well.
They were all to travel across the crossroad, up past the path that led to the Elven kingdom and up the Northern road to the Ventricala path where fierce battles were raging.
The Lacertians had pushed forward, allowing for Horridum to sneak behind them and enter the borderlands without the soldiers of Verrenum's knowledge. Ackley was in a deep state of meditation, trying to conjure up an idea on what to do with the fact King Gila was with them, and had the witch Francine held captive. It was during rest in the middle of the night when the wizard was watching the stars fall from the sky that Bonasus the bisonite approached him.
"You can't sleep either?" He asked Ackley, staring up at the stars as well.
"No, I tend to just sleep when I'm tired. I was never able to get into a routine. What about you?" The wizard asked.
"I kept having these nightmares." Bonasus answered, and then the wizard felt a change in the air. It suddenly became cooler. It was as if the sky had darkened also and the wind picked up swaying the trees and echoing through the landscape. He turned

to look at Bonasus whose eyes had turned completely black and was smiling. Ackley pulled his sword out and stepped back in fear.
The demon possessing Bonasus laughed. "Oh Ackley, how good it is to see you again!"
"Scurrain!" He retorted.
Scurrain possessing Bonasus laughed. "You know exactly how to get the witch back and banish Gila from these lands." The demon said, loud enough so that one of the soldiers heard. He looked up at Ackley wondering what was going on. The mage told him with a hand gesture to stay where he was, and began leading Scurrain away from the ears of others.
"Fuck!" Ackley exclaimed, knowing the demon's trickery.
"How are you even here?" The wizard asked.
"The bisonite died in Pheronia. The witch brought him back. I just latched on, knowing your destinies were intertwined." Scurrain answered, who looked even more evil than Ackley had remembered.
"So, make your final wish wizard." Scurrain said, clearly loving the predicament Ackley was in, "You know she'll be tortured if you don't. And Gila will kill them all, maybe even you, before you get your only protection from me."
Ackley stared at Scurrain who continued, "Yes. I know of your plan to get a paradisian stone."
The demon laughed, "Do you really think that's going to work?"

Ackley stayed silent. He clenched his jaw, lifted his head and stared at the demon, and then he smiled and began to laugh.
As much as he hated Scurrain, he couldn't help but admire his genius. The wizard sat down on a boulder, and then he made his third and final wish to the demon.
Gila was cast out of Francine, rapidly returning to the prison cell, and she returned to her form in Verrenum, screaming.
Scurrain was gone and Bonasus looked around confused as to where he was, and bewildered by the witches' screams. Mehinnerst awoke and rushed to the witches' tent.
"What the curse is going on?" He asked, opening it as she rushed out towards him.
"King Gila, he was here! He possessed me. He trapped me in Lacertia. He knows of our plan. He knows everything!" She exclaimed, gripping at Mehinnerst's cloak.
The others began to wake up at the commotion.
"If he possessed you, then a part of you must have possessed him." Ackley interjected, as he approached.
"What's going on Ackley?" Mehinnerst asked.
Realising he was right, suddenly Francine saw the inside of Gila's head. She remembered it all. She knew of his plans to enter the borderlands at the Ventricala path, and she saw the demon Scurrain ejecting Gila from her form because of Ackley's wish.

"You saved me. You used your final wish on me!" She said, "Thank you!" And she pushed herself onto the wizard and kissed his cheek.
"You're welcome." He replied.
"You need to tell me what happened, Ackley." Mehinnerst ordered, still confused about what had gone on, "We are a team, we deserve to know."
"Ok." The wizard replied, and he began to tell them his story.
"I was in a very different place mindwise. I was 24, and my daughter was ill. No magic could help her. I tried everything. I searched every library, read every book on magic there was. I begged every other mage I could find to help us but none of them could. I was already lost to the world, I mean, you know what I was like, anarchistic, nihilistic, my life didn't really mean much to me, I felt like my beautiful child was the only decent thing I had ever done, and she was dying, and I came across the darkest magic you could find. A grimoire that had spells on how to conjure those in Danmur and to do deals with them."
"You did a deal with a demon?" Mehinnerst asked.
"Yes." Ackley answered.
"And you got three wishes, in exchange for eternal slavery in Danmur when you die?" Mehinnerst asked.
"Yes. Well the first was obvious. I wished for my daughter to live a long and happy life. She can never go to Danmur now. If any of them try to take her, the contract will be broken, if a contract is broken then all contracts are broken, their God wouldn't allow it." Ackley answered.

"And the second?" Mehinnerst asked.
Ackley began laughing, "I asked to know what was wrong with my life, for the knowledge of the Gods. And of the infinite. I didn't know what I had done at the time but I began to get what I asked for." He answered.
"That's why you're so powerful, and survived in the borderlands, and why you changed." Francine said.
Ackley smiled wryly.
"And the third, I just used now. Show him." Ackley said to Francine, and he let the witch enter his mind and she saw it all, putting her hand on Mehinnerst's head so he could see as well.
They saw the fight between Gila and Ackley, and how he had reversed time, and then his conversation with the demon possessing Bonasus, and the wish he made to cast the lizard king out and bring the witch Francine back.
"That's why you want the paradisian stone, because it repels demons among other things." Mehinnerst said.
Ackley nodded.
"Leriskil wants me. He is weary of my deal, because of the gnosis I gained." Ackley said.
"I'm not surprised Ackley. If you sold your soul for the knowledge of the infinite then your powers could rival not only his own powers but the Father's who sent him to rule over the underworld."
"I don't know about that." Ackley replied, "It comes in waves. Like I just know how to do things, like time travel sometimes, or manipulating the trees and

animals, the elements, stuff like that. I don't know how powerful I'll become. It's strange to me."
"Thank you for saving her." Mehinnerst said and he turned to Francine, "What was it like?" He asked, so she touched his head and showed him the lacertian cell she had been trapped in, and the castle, and the markings on the wall.
"I can never go back. I can never be a spy again. I'm sorry." Francine said.
"It's ok, I understand." Mehinnerst replied.
"The rook, Kawmdo, he betrayed the revolution. They're all dead." She declared.
"Well we have our own battle to fight now. We can still reach the path in time and stop Gila's soldiers from carving their way through the borderlands." Mehinnerst said, "Get some rest, we'll travel hard when the sun rises."

King Gila marched out of the witches' prison cell slamming the door with rage and up the corridors towards his council room. Some of the other prisoners pleaded with him for release but he moved straight past them, feeling no empathy or any other emotions but greed and hatred.
He was fascinated by what the wizard Ackley had done. They had a demon with them! A demon that the overlord had deemed too evil for paradise and sent to rule over Danmur instead. They really were evil in Verrenum!
He sent for Kawmdo and the rest of his council and headed to his throne room. Sitting on the huge gold

chair, he scratched at the metal on the armrests and suddenly began feeling very content with the Overlord's plan.
The fact the Verrenum Wizards were travelling with a demon was a sure sign to him that they were evil, and would lose. His council began to enter, but all stayed silent, knowing the King wouldn't need them to tell him anything. He would already know of the Rook Horridum's plans, the Anaki and the soldiers carving a way through the borderlands and around the battles at Ventricala, and they were right to think this.

Francine, who was fascinated by the gnomes, allowed Dosigene and a few others to ride with her up the Northern road. They were the most magical of creatures. They disappeared at times and came back with huge feasts for themselves. They carved strange machines out of wood, making musical instruments and weapons. One of them even built a small contraption which enabled him to fly, and they all talked about Ackley, and his many adventures in the borderlands.
"You talk of him as if he is a celebrity." Laughed the witch.
"Ah but he is exactly that to us Francine." Dosigene replied.
"Yeah, exactly that!" Called out the others.
"Why do you like him so much?" She asked, as the horse trotted along and the gnomes began growing in size ever so slightly so they could communicate more efficiently.

"A few of us were captured by the mermaids."
Dosigene said.
"Yes, mermaids!" Repeated the others.
"Sirens!" One called out.
"Yes, the sirens!" Dosigene shouted, "Well we were trapped in cages when the wizard escaped, and he risked his own life to set us free."
"Yes! He set us free!" Shouted the others.
"Yeah, he did that for me too." She replied, looking over at the wizard who was walking alongside the soldiers with his hood up, and his eyes on the forest. Just like her he preferred shadows and insects, or shadows and gnomes, in his case.
"We were trapped and being tortured and he saved us all." Dosigene said.
"Yes, he saved us all." Said the other gnomes turning and nodding at each other in agreement.
"And he took us with him back to the borderlands and he let us live with him, and we built a new home there with him."
Dosigene said.
"Yes, a new home." Agreed one of the other gnomes, nodding his head.
"More food! More vegetables to grow! And freedom!" Shouted another.
"Yes, freedom!" Some of the others shouted.
Francine smiled.
"We are nearly there." She said as the others began hearing the battles being fought at Ventricala.
The western city of the elves was beginning to appear on their left, a great port city, where the Elves

controlled most of the seas, and kept the invading Lacertian ships at bay.
They all stared in wonder at it. It was a coastal town and the path they were on was high up amongst the hills so they could see almost all of it quite clearly. They passed the city and began approaching the roaring of the battle where the Rook Graipant was waiting for them, with an army to block the Lacertian advance through the borderlands.
There were dragons fighting each other in the sky, with Lacertians, men and elves all riding on their backs. And miles and miles of soldiers attacking one another in a constant sea of battle. It was the most intricate and destructive thing all of them had ever seen. Mehinnerst led them through the army camps to the Rook's tent, where he led Francine and Ackley inside.

The Lacertians of operation roadkill had travelled a few miles into the borderlands carving a path as they did. They had hacked away at the trees and plants, they had crushed the grass with their feet and left a trail of marks for their return.
"Valestine, what is it?" The rook Horridum asked, who was the only one riding on horseback. The Anaki leader Valestine had suddenly stopped and crouched down, his eyes peered around.
"The land, it's beginning to change." The Anaki answered. He could feel it. This fog of dread had surrounded him.

"We're going too deep, we need to stay as close as we can to the Ventricala path, while at the same time as deep in as we can go, but look." He said, and he pointed to the ground ahead which was beginning to swirl.
"We've angered the land by coming too deep. We've angered the Overlord. We need to move back." He exclaimed.
Valestine began moving backwards. He ordered the other Anaki to do the same but as they did the ground began swallowing some of them and the soldiers. The rook Horridum turned his horse and began riding towards the back of the troops knocking some down and out of his way but the ground rose and he was knocked off his horse. He got up, flustered and returned to it. He shouted angrily, "Carve a road closer to the Ventricala path men, we've gone too deep."

"Mehinnerst. Good to see you." Rook Graipaint said, as he shook the wizard's hand.
"And Francine, great to see you too." The rook turned towards Ackley.
"And is this him? Is this Ackley?" He asked Mehinnerst.
"Yes, Rook Graipaint, this is the wizard Ackley. He has agreed to help us on our mission." Mehinnerst answered.
"Nice to meet you, Ackley. Verrenum is in your debt, please join us." Said the rook smiling and gesturing

towards his table which was surrounded by bishops with stuffy, serious looks on their faces.
Ackley, who had noticed Dosigene and the gnomes had sneaked into the tent, smiled and said " So is there a toilet here? I really need to have a massive shit."
Laughing, the wizard turned back time and the three entered the tent again.
"Mehinnerst. Good to see you." Rook Graipaint said as he shook the wizard's hand.
"And Francine, great to see you too." The rook turned towards Ackley. "And is this him? Is this Ackley?" He asked Mehinnerst.
"Yes, Rook Graipaint, this is the wizard Ackley. He has agreed to help us on our mission." Mehinnerst answered.
"Nice to meet you, Ackley. Verrenum is in your debt, please join us." Said the rook gesturing towards his table which was surrounded by bishops with stuffy, serious looks on their faces.
Ackley winked at Dosigene who was trying to control his laughter. Ackley began laughing.
"Rook Graipaint, this is my own rook, the gnome Dosigene. He is here to help." He said, and the wizard gestured to some books on the table where the gnome appeared from and walked towards where Ackley had approached.
"They know the borderlands even better than I." Ackley declared.

"Yes, we know the borderlands very well, very well!" The other gnomes repeated as they came out from their hiding places.
"Great, well the more help we have, the better. We don't know whether King Gila has ordered any Lacertian's into the borderlands yet." The rook replied.
"Yes, he has." Mehinnerst said, "King Gila plans to do exactly what King Mindsley predicted. He is sending a troop through to carve a path around us."
"He has sent his Anaki with Rook Horridum to lead." Francine said.
"How do you know this?" The rook asked.
"He possessed me." The witch answered.
The rook and especially the bishops looked shocked by this.
"Oh don't worry, he has been ejected and I won't give him another chance to. The revolution in Lacertia failed. King Gila knew of it all along. He is a mage himself." The witch said.
"He's a mage!?" Rook Graipaint asked.
"Yes, and a very powerful one as well." The witch answered.
"What else have you discovered?" The rook asked.
"Well, not to travel by Pheronia." Laughed Francine.
"Pheronia. The mermaid city. I thought it was a myth!" The rook replied.
"No, it's very real." Mehinnerst said.
"We need to leave with an army straight away and cut them off here." Declared Mehinnerst and the wizard pointed to a spot on the map, "Ackley will guide us, for a paradisian stone."

The rook nodded.
"I need two." Ackley interjected, "The bisonite will need one as well to eject the demon in him."
"We need two paradisian stones." Mehinnerst said to the rook.
"Yes, consider it done." Rook Graipaint replied, and he ordered one of his bishops to fetch them.
"Your army awaits Mehinnerst. I'll make sure you get the stones before you leave. Bring yourself back, you hear?"
"Goodbye Seth." Mehinnerst said, while nodding, "I'll see you when I get back." And he shook the Rook's hand, and then left with the others.

Mehinnerst went to collect his army, while Francine, Ackley and Dosigene joined the other soldiers ready to take them to their entry point in the borderlands.
"It should be the same. Not much difference." Ackley declared.
"Yes! The same! Not much difference." Repeated the gnomes.
"We are near the coast though." Ackley said.
"Yes, the coast!" Repeated the gnomes.
"And the elves." Said Dosigene.
"Yes, the elves!" Repeated another gnome.
"We should let Robin lead then." Ackley said, referring to his white wolf.
"Why?" Francine asked, trying to keep up.
Ackley and Dosigene looked at each other.
"Because she used to live with them." The wizard answered, which made the gnomes laugh.

"I want you to do something Francine. I need you to understand." Ackley said.
"Understand what?" The witch asked.
"Why you need to stay close to us." The wizard answered, referring to himself and the gnomes, and he stopped in front of her, and he dismantled the spell that was keeping her out of his mind for a few moments and she didn't just see his own experiences in the borderlands but that of Verrenum's itself. She was connecting directly to it. She saw all the way back to the black ages, thousands of years before where soldiers would enter and be swallowed up by the wildness of the borderlands, and the grey ages right up until the white ages, thousands of years of memories. Then it stopped abruptly and she understood the danger they were getting into. She understood the depth of respect the wizard had for the land and in return it had let him survive, and that she needed to be this way too.
The group joined the other soldiers where Bonasus was waiting, not with the black eyes of Scurrain but the yellow eyes of Leriskil. When the soldiers noticed this they scurried away from Bonasus in fear. Hoodrow attempted to speak to him and call the bisonite back but the horror of Leriskil was so much that he fell to the ground ill. He clambered away too. Francine, stood in awe staring at the God of Danmur in the bisonite's form, as it approached Ackley who had stalled. The gnomes stared at him in hatred and defiance but even for them with all of their genius

Leriskil could not be outwitted, and they feared him too.
"You may get them stones to eject me wizard, but there is no escaping what you owe." Leriskil said, and even possessing Bonasus all of them could see how beautiful he was, and how terrifying. He moved like a snake and got closer to Ackley, who was for the first time any had seen him, visibly afraid.
"I am the Father's favourite. What I do is because he allows me to Ackley. It is his will. I am the son of God, remember that." Leriskil said.
"And I am a son of the infinite, I am the son of the way. My parent is the creator of yours. You remember that." Ackley snarled back, and he gripped his sword, and Pyra began blazing beside him in full woman form aiming an arrow at the God of Danmur. Leriskil saw this, that the arrow would hit him and not the bisonite and he laughed once in defiance.
"Soon." Leriskil said, as Mehinnerst began approaching, carrying the Paradisian stones in his pocket. The God of Danmur and the demon Scurrain went back to Danmur and Bonasus took control of his form again. There was an eerie silence that made Mehinnerst nervous as he approached.
The wizard Ackley rubbed his face. He paced back and forth a bit, angry, clenching his jaw, and then he turned and greeted Mehinnerst, taking one of the stones and passing the other to Bonasus.
"I need to plan our route. I need to discuss it with the gnomes, alone. We'll be back when it's ready." Ackley said, and he led his group; Pyra, the gnomes and

Robin just beyond the ears of the others, close to the forest.
"What was that about?" Mehinnerst asked Francine, who touched his head and showed him everything.

The group had entered the borderlands. Robin, the white wolf led the way, and Ackley who had morphed into a black wolf went with her. The gnomes and Pyra stayed with Mehinnerst and his army.
They had travelled about 3 miles into the forest when the wolves began heading westwards. Both had caught the scent of the Lacertian invaders. The pair began running through the forest making sure not to outrun the others when they came across the Lacertians carving a road through it.
Ackley morphed back into wizard form and sent Robin back to signal that the Lacertian's had been found. He thought back to when he was a child and his Father would teach him to hunt rabbits, learning how to be completely silent and sneak up on the prey and then, to be as ferocious as possible for both the rabbit and his own sake, just like a tiger. They kill quickly, so that the deer will die as fast as possible and so that itself doesn't get any unnecessary kicks.
It was time for the army to lead now, the wizard thought as Mehinnerst came to his side.
"What's your plan?" Ackley asked.
"Let them come this way, have our archers surprise them and then we take care of the rest." Mehinnerst answered, peering through the gaps in the trees at the Lacertian army, "Come, we need to move back."

The wizards sneaked back to where the rest of their army was waiting. The gnomes allowed Ackley to see them in their hiding places. They held their infamous crossbows but with much more dangerous spells than turning their victims into butterflies.
Ackley got into position with Mehinnerst and Francine and waited for the battle to begin.

Valestine and the rest of the Anaki crept forward. They felt another ambush awaiting, so they moved in a slightly south direction as they walked.
The Rook Horridum led the army behind them who were still cutting through the bushes and stamping the plants into the ground.
Suddenly Valestine saw the witch Francine's white and black face in his mind and realised that she had been leading them. The other Anaki saw it too and they began pulling out their weapons. The Rook's horse reared up and neighed as it noticed the archers all around them. It was hit with one of the gnomes' crossbows and throwing Horridum to the ground, he watched on in disarray as a huge eggshell began to grow around the animal trapping it inside.
"To arms!" Shouted the Lacertian Rook, as arrows and fire began hitting the army. The Anaki had already pulled their shields, joined and created a metal shell around themselves.
The Lacertian's created a wall with their shields on either side of them, and so Mehinnerst ordered the others to attack. The soldiers rushed forwards and began ferociously kicking the Lacertian's shields and

smashing at them with their swords and axes. The Lacertian's split and began attacking back.
Ludlow the butterfly attacked from above, whizzing through the air and carrying soldiers up into the sky only to drop them after. Lacertian archers tried to shoot arrows at him but he spun out of their way and hid amongst the trees, clutching to the branches, returning when their focus was elsewhere.
Angrard the dwarf was swinging his axe and snapping Lacertian necks with ease when a Lacertian mage threw him back with magical force. The dwarf hid behind a tree and the verrenum soldiers around him who moved forwards began getting huge splits and stabs through their skin from the mage's magical power.
The bark around the tree began hitting him like shrapnel as the mage proceeded ripping away at his hiding place. Bits of wood lodged into his cheek so he rushed backwards.
Tristan the mage moved past him, and the two wizards began firing their magic at one another. The Lacertian mage's head was suddenly ripped clean off and Tristan moved forward to attack the Lacertian soldiers.
Mayscott and Bonfield were barraging through the Lacertians, smacking and crushing them against trees and cutting them down with their huge swords.
"I'm killing the most!" Bonfield shouted. "No! I'm killing the most!" Replied Mayscott as he lifted a Lacertian soldier on his sword and threw him at the others who were proceeding.

Bonasus was swinging his huge axe with horrendous violence at the Lacertian's around him. One of the Anaki noticed him, and in need of a challenge after killing so many Verrenum soldiers he came on Bonasus. The two began fighting and although the bisonite put up one hell of a fight, the anaki cut his hand and kicked him to the floor as he dropped his axe.
He was about to kill the bisonite when Hoodrow shot him with one of the gnome crossbows and the Anaki was turned into stone. Bonasus began laughing and picking his axe back up, he continued fighting.
Pyra was in full burning form. She raged through any Lacertian soldiers that attacked her like an inferno. She was even killing the Anaki with ease until one threw a magical cube at her. It opened near her feet and the fire spirit screamed as she was dragged inside of it.
Hoodrow seeing this rushed towards it, he grabbed the cube as the wolf Robin leapt over him and tore into the Anaki's throat. The wolf turned and he jumped on her back and continued firing his arrows. Suddenly he felt the cube burning in his pocket. He took it out and threw it away as Pyra burst out of it even more enraged than before. She hated being held captive! She took her bow and arrow of fire and began pulling back harder on it. The little orc watched on in awe as she sent arrows that exploded on impact burning dozens of Lacertians with every shot, and sending them flying through the air.

Francine was dancing through the Lacertian army. She didn't use a sword. She turned to smoke or dodged any blows that came near her. She tapped a soldier and set him on fire. She spun around another and snapped his neck. She came to an anaki and rushed in smoke form into his mouth, making him hit the floor and cough up the black liquid she was pouring into his lungs.
A Lacertian mage put out his hand and exorcised her from him and the two began throwing elements at each other. The Lacertian used sand and she used fire, until she morphed into a murder of crows and swarmed him, pecking at his eyes, cutting open his skin and making him run blindly into a tree. She then returned to her witch form, picked up a discarded sword and impaled him to the ground.
Ackley rushed towards Valestine. He threw the Anaki leader up into the air, spinning him and sending him flying, but the Lacertian sent his tongue out and gripped a branch on a tree with it. He swung back and drop kicked the wizard backwards. Ackley went flying through the air and tumbled over the forest floor amongst the dirt and leaves. He was bleeding, and he wiped his face with his hand leaving downward lines of blood like war paint on it and stared defiantly into the Anaki leader's eyes.
Valestine rushed him and as Ackley stood up he pulled out his sword and the two began fighting. Their swords clashed. Ackley put out his hand and ripped the Lacertian's skin with magical power. Valestine recoiled and lashed at the wizard's face with his

tongue which knocked Ackley back and left a gash from his cheek to his ear.
The wizard rushed forward again with his sword but could not better Valestine in this way as the Lacertian was too practised in the art of swordplay, so the wizard opened up the ground beneath him, as Verrenum and the borderlands were on his side. Valestine fell up to his waist, trapped in the earth, so the wizard stuck his sword right through his heart, and then swung it round and cut off his head.
Ackley took a step back, he was breathing heavily, he took a vial from his pocket and began covering his wounds with a powerful green poultice. He then took another vial and drank it. The wizard kept moving behind the battle lines healing the sick he could find with his potions until he looked up and saw Mehinnerst fighting the Rook Horridum.
The rook whose armour was covered in markings that repelled magic was sword fighting with Mehinnerst. Ackley moved towards them as Horridum parried away Mehinnerst's sword and then pierced the wizard through the chest.
The Lacertian gripped the Verrenum mage bit into his neck like a vampire and then threw him to the ground. That's when Ackley got the feeling from Verrenum to start manipulating the trees and the earth. Suddenly the Lacertian soldiers began getting gripped by tree branches, and hung up into the air. They began to flee as the plants wrapped around them, crushing them and poisoning them. Ackley moved the earth with his powers and it began swallowing the remainder of the

Lacertian army. Even the Anaki were shocked by his power and fled.
The rook Horridum looked around in anger. He saw his army either dying or fleeing and he cursed them all. He would not return to Gila as a coward! He rushed towards Ackley and the two began sword fighting. He pushed Ackley backwards with his strength and ferocity but the wizard parried away his advances.
"No magic will work on me wizard, you'll have to beat me the normal way." The Lacertian spat out in a mocking tone. Ackley continued fighting until a tree swung its branch around and pierced Rook Horridum's chest.
Ackley, shocked by this, as it wasn't his own magic that moved it, looked up at the tree whose bark was shifting. He saw a face smiling in the wood and then, it was gone again. It was Verrenum. He leaned back against another tree and looked up at the sky, and he saw another face in the blue watching over him. The battle was over.

Francine was crouched over Mehinnerst trying to stop the bleeding and doing what she could to save him. Ackley approached and Tristan turned to him and said "You can save him right? Just go back in time."
"Ackley." Dosigene said, "It's time. Tell them how many times you have fought this battle."
Tristan looked at Dosigene and then back at Ackley.
"How many times?" Francine asked.

The wizard looked around at the trees, then back at the witch.
"About a hundred." He answered.
"Now ask him how many times he has been close to death because of it." Said the gnome.
"How many?" Francine asked, as she stood up and stepped towards Ackley.
"Show her." Dosigene said.
Ackley sighed, and he let the Verrenum witch enter his mind and she saw him getting hit with arrows, torn up by the Lacertian mages power, and stabbed with their swords, using his powers of time travel just in time to fight the battle again. She saw that no matter how many times he tried, Mehinnerst would always die, and sometimes herself as well.
Francine turned to Mehinnerst who had seen it too, and he smiled.
"No more Ackley, that's an order. Let me go." Mehinnerst said, clutching his wounds.
"I can figure out a way." Ackley said, crouching down and putting pressure on the wizard's wound.
Mehinnerst shook his head, "No. You've done enough. Some things you cannot change. I'll die with my men, for Verrenum. I'm ok with that. You know, I don't know as much as you about magic, or even Verrenum, but I'm pretty sure you can escape Danmur by continuing in this way."
Ackley looked away.
"But it's not just the deal. The things I did. The mage I was." Ackley said, and he began remembering his past and all the terrible things he had done in his

youth, all the mistakes he had made and the violent wizard he had become, the dark magic and spirits he had conjured.
"Just use the spell you haven't used yet." Mehinnerst whispered, as he edged closer to death.
"What's that? What spell?" Ackley asked.
Mehinnerst smiled.
"Redemption." He whispered.
Ackley began tearing up. He clenched his jaw and wiped a tear from his eye.
Mehinnerst put his hand to his chest and ripped off the necklace he was wearing and passed it to Ackley.
"Redemption." He whispered, and then his head fell to the side, and he died.
Ackley stood up, he looked at the necklace and then he put it in his pocket.
"Will you do one more thing for us?" Francine asked, noticing what Mehinnerst had given the wizard.
"Yes, what is it?" He answered.
"Come back with us to speak to the rook." Francine said.
"Sure." He concluded.

The mages and soldiers had returned to the army camps just beyond the battle of Ventricala. They were tired from the battle and dropped their weapons and rested.
Francine and Tristan led Ackley into Rook Graipaint's tent where King Mindsley had arrived. He smiled at the mages.

"What news from the borderlands? Did you stall the Lacertian invasion? Where is Mehinnerst?" The King asked as he greeted them.
Francine sat down and looked away. Tristan began to speak.
"The Lacertians have been neutralised. We killed them and the rest fled." He stated.
"And Mehinnerst?" Mindsley enquired.
"He fell, sir." Tristan answered.
"Oh no." The king retorted, and he sat down as well, rubbing his head in his hand.
"I'd like a full report please Tristan, or Francine. Which one of you will succeed him?" The King asked.
"He will." Said Tristan, turning towards Ackley.
"What!?" Ackley exclaimed.
"He passed you his necklace Ackley. The one the King gave him to show his authority as the mage rook." Francine said.
"I'm honoured, but I don't want to lead." Ackley said.
"Only a true leader doesn't want to lead Ackley." Francine said, "That's why he chose you. It's time for you to come home. Stop running from who you are." She stood up and embraced him.
"Please. Verrenum needs you. I need you." She whispered in his ear.
"I have your next assignment if you'd like to hear it." Rook Graipaint commented, carrying some papers.
"What is it?" Ackley asked.
Francine smiled.
"Well Ackley, have you ever heard of the King of the rats?" Asked the rook.

Printed in Great Britain
by Amazon

67709908R00088